We call everything a river here.
We're that kind of people.
                    Richard Brautigan
                    In Watermelon Sugar

Jeffrey Dunn was spawned in Chicago and raised in a Pittsburgh rearing tank. Once out to sea, he swam among various schools, earning a BA in English, an MA in Education, and a Ph.D. in English Literature and Culture Studies. He returned to the fresh water of parochial and public schools and taught English to smolts. He was transplanted to Washington State in 1993 and later to the Little Spokane River Drainage in 2002. Washington State's OSPI, ESD 101, and Education Association have judged Jeffrey's teaching to be Premium, which is to say a sea-fresh odor, bright and clear eyes, bright red gills, and a bright and natural body cavity. His teaching also has no fin damage or tail loss.

Jeffrey writes a good bit.

1. *Dream Fishing the Little Spokane* is published through Jeffrey's Inchitensee imprint and distributed by IngramSpark. eBook and audio copies are planned and may be available through Amazon in 2018.

2. *Radio Free Olympia* is about a young man who pirate-radio broadcasts spirits in Washington's Olympic Mountains and a young woman who raises cranberries and runs Wildsisters, a women's roadhouse. Of course, the two find each other during the soon-to-come Pacific Rim Apocalypse. Someday maybe Jeffrey will publish this one.

3. *William S. Burroughs and Technologizing Literary Studies in the Industrial Age* 1991 is Jeffrey's dissertation which can be found through the University of Minnesota's dissertation services.

4. Lots of other print and electronic stuff is cast like milt upon a redd.

Dream Fishing

The Little Spokane

a novel by

JEFFREY DUNN

INCHITENSEE

First published in 2017 by Inchitensee
11707 North Waikiki Road
Spokane, WA 99218
inchitensee@gmail.com

ISBN 13: 978-0-9993339-0-7
ISBN 10: 0-9993339-0-9
Library of Congress Cataloguing-in-Publication Data
is available from the Library of Congress

Distributed by IngramSpark

Cover photograph by Jamie Shepherd 2016. Courtesy
of the photographer.

First Printing

For Jamie, Wilson, and Beck
Shepherd
        David Strellec
        Camas and Seth Lockwood

CONTENTS

THE COVER FOR

DREAM FISHING

THE LITTLE SPOKANE

(PART ONE)

AXE NOTCHED

LOVINGLY FOR YOU

The cover of *Dream Fishing the Little Spokane* is a digital image taken on an uncharacteristically cool summer afternoon on the peninsula between the Spokane and Little Spokane Rivers. The soundtrack playing off camera is a lawn mower working against the effects of an underground sprinkler system on hardware store turf grasses. Someone has declared war on native bunch grass. Someone really wants to form a more perfect union at the expense of the rebel vegetation in these parts.

The eye is looking through a knothole in a one-hundred-fifty year-old barn. This dogtrot-styled, log structure is the second oldest manmade building in Spokane County. In 1925 William S. Lewis wrote this description:

> About half a mile south of the mouth of the Little Spokane and toward the Spokane River there was then standing a log building built of peeled logs. The roof timbers were fastened on with wooden pegs and the roof, of cedar shakes, was

also fastened on with wooden
pegs. The building was built up
with a log enclosure at each end
and a threshing floor in the
middle. At that time it had a
floor made of logs hewn by hand.
On this floor the Indians threshed
their grain, either by using a
flail or by putting in two or
three cayuse ponies to trample the
grain out.

The log ends are axe notched, not
dovetailed, to provide stability. Dovetailing
required more time and effort and angled away
intruding rain. Axe notched ends were the
manual windows on a Ford Econoline Van. "Don'
need no frills to take away from my bottom
line, if y'know what I mean." "Are you sure
you wouldn't want to upgrade the carpets or
sound system? Maybe add an air conditioner?"
"Just more money for you and less for me.
Thank y'kindly, but no."
    Fairly recently some school children were
directed to put a new shake shingle roof on
top. The workmanship was very professional.
The shakes were factory milled to exacting
standards. The joists and roofline are still
dead level. The new roof looks like an old tin
type of a dog soldier with a U. S. cavalry hat
set on his head. The young warrior has that
serious expression that all faces have on old
images. He had to sit a long time for his
picture to develop, and you have to wonder
what he was thinking all the time he sat
waiting for the magic to take his soul. No
doubt he thought some about his loved ones,
his father and mother, his brothers,
sisters, and cousins, and this one particular
girl that he couldn't get out of his thoughts,
a burning ember, a coal he kept blowing on
until he could have that girl. She was just

like the hat he took from that soldier when he
cut the soldier's throat with the beaver tail
dag knife he traded for at the trading post.

Historians are pretty sure James, Peavine
Jimmy, Walton built what has become this log
monument. At twenty Jimmy floated like
cottonwood fluff from Pennsylvania's turnip
still country to California's American River
gold fields and then from British Columbia's
Fraser River gold fields down to this very
spot. He was mild-mannered, a crack-shot, an
accomplished carpenter, and occasionally a
partaker of "the devil's rum" and "firewater."

It also could be said that Peavine Jimmy
was "regulated by the wildness of the
neighbourhood." This is what J. Hector St.
John Crevecouer said was true of all Western
Americans. He said this was so because "men
are like plants." Jimmy was dubbed "Peavine"
because he fed *Vicia americana* to his frontier
trail horses as winter fodder. Like Jimmy,
peavines spring up in wild places from road
banks to swampy woods and open meadows to
burned forests.

To the north and south of the cover for
Dream Fishing the Little Spokane, people come
to launch and retrieve their boats. To the
south kayaks and canoes are collected after a
leisurely float. It's against the law to fish
from the Little Spokane's banks. Here the
Little Spokane is an amusement park's lazy
river. To the north power boats both big and
small are launched into the larger Spokane
River's slack water behind the Long Lake Dam.
The free flow of the Spokane River has been
stopped in the service of power. Electricity
is produced to toast five-year-old Suzie's
root beer toaster pastry. Gasoline is burned
by the 50 horsepower, 4-stroke outboard motor
which drives a boat and skier across the
water's glassy surface. The Spokane River
offers little resistance, biding its time. It

3

was a lake during the ice age. It can be a lake now, too.

No evidence exists that Chief Spokane Garry ever met Peavine Jimmy, although Garry walked this very spot as a boy. Before Peavine Jimmy the junction of the Spokane and Little Spokane Rivers was a fishing village and a Hudson's Bay trading post. Later Garry built the first school in the region on the other side of the Spokane River.

It was Chief Spokane Garry who once said, "Why are these Americans alive now? Why were they not hanged?"

THE COVER FOR

DREAM FISHING

THE LITTLE SPOKANE

(PART TWO)

WORDS IN MY MOUTH

This child's letter was sent to the Little
Spokane. The child signed his letter Slough-
keetcha. He is now known as Chief Spokane
Garry. His Spokane name is reported to have
been lost. Don't believe everything you hear.

When the letter reached the Little
Spokane, Slough-keetcha's words bloomed like
pine drops on the forest floor. The rains had
stopped for the summer, and then the rains
fell in a July downpour. Up came the child's
words. After that the rains stopped for a very
long time.

This letter was almost lost to history. It
was saved by the Church Missionary Society in
1829 when it was published in their *Missionary
Register* for MDCCCXXIX (Vol. 17). It was
published in London by L.B. Seely & Sons. You
have to admit, God has some sense of humor.

> My Dear Father and Mother—I am
> very glad that I can write to you,
> and that I can tell you that I am
> well. I have never been sick since
> I came to this place; and I have
> always had food to eat and clothes
> to put on. I can now read much of
> that book that the Great Spirit

5

has given to the White People, to
tell them what they must do, so
that when they die they may go to
the good country. This book tells
us that there is a time coming,
when Indians, as well as White
Men, shall know what the Great
Spirit has said in this book, and
what they ought to do to please
Him. I wish, my Dear Father and
Mother, that you, my Sisters and
Brothers, and all my Country-
people, knew these things. Give my
love to my Uncle Chongulloosoon,
and to all my Aunts; and I would
thank you to send me a deer-skin.
The great Illemechum whom you saw
before, takes this Letter. Be good
to the White People, for they are
good to us.

Your son
Slough-keetcha

LITTLE SPOKANE WELCOME WAGON

Dear New Neighbor,

You're new to our neighborhood. I thought I'd
stop by and introduce myself. We should get to
know one another now that we're neighbors. I
was going to get a grocery store pie, you
know, one of those they bake up and put out
with the other baked goods. I didn't, though.
I changed my mind. I was a bit embarrassed
because you never know how long those pies
have been sitting out. And they aren't really
good, at least not like a really good homemade
pie. Of course, some homemade pies are awful.
Sometimes they have cardboard crusts, and
sometimes the fruit all falls out, the juice
running all over the plate. It can get me
really depressed, you know? So, I thought
maybe a grocery store pie, an apple might be
really good, would be a nice get-to-know-you
gift. But then I got embarrassed, like I said
already, and I didn't get anything.

> Kindest Regards,
> *Mister White*

Dear Mister White,

From what I can gather, you've lived here for
quite awhile, all your life, in fact. You
might say you're a native. I've never lived
anywhere for any length of time. I don't know
what it's like to be FROM somewhere, if you
know what I mean. I don't suppose you would,

what with you being born in the Little
Spokane, but it seems like I've moved every
few years or so. I don't know, maybe I just
want to see what's around the next corner or
beyond that next horizon. Am I restless? Do I
have a problem with commitment? Might I
benefit from settling down and putting down
some roots? All good questions. All very good
questions.

Lookin' forward,
Will Black

NOMINATING VIPER BUGLOSS
FOR
THE NOXIOUS WEED BOARD

Viper Bugloss was an unkempt, mostly silent, scavenger of indeterminate age, the fly amanita at the bottom of a whiskey glass.

He was a fatwa issued against anyone possessing a shred of humanity. He was a murderboat upon which the 5000 innocent women and children of the revolutionary French city of Nantes were sailed out into the Loire River and drowned. He was more than the five rodent hairs and one-hundred-and-fifty bug parts the government allows in a pound of peanut butter.

He was the reason things disappeared from campgrounds throughout the Little Spokane watershed. One morning a hippie-chick mom all tie-dye sweatshirt and do-rag is cooking bacon in a Bear Creek campsite just off Mount Spokane Road. She turns her back on the hot cast iron skillet to scoop some coffee grounds into the drip filter. When she turns back to the fire, the skillet and bacon have vanished into the gray jay air.

Then again, forty miles north off Buck Creek Road and bushwhacking up Boyer Mountain, a deer hunter with his bolt-action 30-06 rifle and bivy bag gets ready to bed down. He suspends his food fifty feet above the forest floor and leaves his axe and boots outside on a downed tree. Now he lays himself down to sleep. Not a twig snaps. Come morning his axe and boots are nowhere to be found.

Spokane, Kalispel, and Coeur d'alene tribal members know Viper Bugloss to be of some indeterminate mixed race. He didn't seem to be an urban Indian, and he certainly didn't belong to anyone's reservation. A few old timers said they'd heard he was the offspring of a French blackrobe and an Upper Spokane. Further down the line there was some illicit Presbyterian missionary liaison. Then to complicate matters a few claimed that he was the three times great grandson of Crow Foot, one of the two Inland Northwest Natives convicted of killing Officer Robert J. Rusk in 1886. Rusk's body was found face down in Deadman Creek just above its confluence with the Little Spokane.

And only occasionally Viper Bugloss showed up at local pow wows. He appeared at these gatherings always sitting on a filthy blanket under a half-dead tree. In these circumstances a certain sort of child was attracted to him. These were the children that some family member brought along and turned loose. These were the kids that were just on their own. "Now get lost. I got me some friends somewhere around here, and we got plans." "But what if ..." "But what? I brought you here didn't I? Now, where did Bobby put that bottle?"

Viper Bugloss always had these wood carvings he fashioned from his imagination. A few people really liked them. A few thought they were statues of tree or water spirits. One or two said they were Giacometti marmots or Bourgeois salamanders.

He also always had a supply of apple jack. He'd give each fairy ring kid a couple of pulls on an old milk bottle filled with the stuff. That would get their interest.

"There's more where this comes from. Go on out and sell some o'these."

"How much?"

"Twenty bucks. Twenty-five if y'can get it. "

"Then what?""

"Come back with the money. We'll settle up. I got a bottle f'r ya of y'r own."

"You bet."

A friend of mine and I once had this great idea one evening. We were walking along the old railroad grade just below the Deer Park Milan Road Bridge. We had a bottle of sweet wine. There was a caddis fly hatch in progress. It was a good time for talking.

"So, I was walking the Painted Rocks Trail along the Little Spokane a few days back, and I came across this plant. It had this hairy stalk and blue, funnel-shaped flowers. I looked it up and found it's called Viper's Bugloss. Isn't there some guy around here with that name?"

"Yeah, I've heard stories. I've never seen him. I think that's the sort of story people make up to scare kids."

"Could be. I read that Viper's Bugloss is listed as a noxious weed in Spokane County. I also read that Spokane County has a Noxious Weed Board. It has five volunteer members. I think we should nominate Viper Bugloss to be on the Spokane County Noxious Weed Board."

"Sounds like a good idea."

I went so far as to find out about the Spokane County Noxious Weed Board. Its website says:

> A state law passed in 1969 mandated that all counties in Washington have a program to combat noxious weeds. The Spokane County Noxious Weed Control Board was established in 1970 and consists of five citizen volunteers who represent five districts that cover the entire

11

county. The Board meets monthly
and provides vision and direction
to the weed control program.

Then I obtained an application for someone
who wanted to volunteer to be on the Board. I
could hear in my head the way Board meetings
would go.

"The Chair recognizes Mr. Lewandowski."

"Thank you Chairman Bugloss. I want to
bring to the attention of the Board an
infestation of Viper's Bugloss. This
infestation is causing grazing issues with my
horses."

"Yes, that can happen," interjects a Board
Member. "Viper's Bugloss is a Class B Noxious
Weed and produces a pyrrolozidine alkaloid
which can cause liver damage, especially in
cattle and horses."

"Thank you Board Member Antonelli."

"But what can we do Chairman Bugloss?"

"Well, Mr. Lewankowski, right now because
most of our noxious weeds have gone to seed,
we've laid off our investigators. Next April
you could file an investigation report, and we
can offer advice based on the level of
infestation."

"So, you are saying, Chairman Bugloss,
that I can't really do anything until Spring?"

"That's right, Mr. Lewandowski. You see,
Viper's Bugloss has already gone to seed, and
we can't deal with the problem until those
seeds germinate. Each Viper's Bugloss plant
produces 500 to 2,000 seeds. Once those
germinate you can apply a residual, broadleaf
herbicide in May or June before the plants go
to seed. Make sure you apply a surfactant,
too, because the hairs on the leaves are so
numerous the herbicide doesn't stay on the
plant well without it. Of course, you can pull
up each plant by hand if you choose. Last
year's plants will have a three foot tap root.

Make sure you wear gloves because the stiff hairs on the stalk cause some pretty nasty skin irritation."

"Okay, I'll wait 'til spring, then."

"Sounds like a plan. If there is no new business, then I, Chairman Bugloss, declare this September meeting of the Spokane County Noxious Weed Control Board adjourned."

I even made a phone call to the Parks Operation Division. These are the folks who are in charge of making government owned places look like people want, places like "large, mountainous open space areas ... developed community parks, off-road vehicle parks and the Centennial Trail."

I found out that I couldn't nominate someone, no matter how deserving, if I couldn't find that person. I couldn't even nominate him if his name were on the very list the Board was charged to control.

I really thought that it was an injustice, you know what I mean? It all seemed to be un-American, taxation without representation and all that, against the Fifth and Fourteenth Amendments. How could the government sentence someone to death by chemical extermination without allowing that person to testify? Where was the equal protection under the law? Are certain plants by definition really three-fifths of a plant?

But since Viper Bugloss' existence was most assuredly, temporarily, legend, I had to forget my plan to nominate him to the Spokane County Noxious Weed Board. I had to be satisfied with postponing my efforts to right this wrong, to make more just all that drains into the Little Spokane.

I had to be content with imagining a very different vision, a much more real and fanciful story. In this epilogue Viper Bugloss is still sitting on that same filthy blanket under that same half-dead tree. Those same fairy ring children are still gathered about.

In this ending the Department of Alcohol, Tobacco, and Firearms and Child Protective Services, all orchestrated by the Department of Homeland Security, descend upon a local pow wow. Folks know something is up when a couple of Bellistic Engineered Armored Response Counter Attack Trucks (BEARCATs) drive right down main street. Folks know something is up when men in riot gear appear with M4a1 assault carbines.

Of course Viper Bugloss is arrested without incident. He is handcuffed and summarily put for safekeeping into the back of a BEARCAT, like Crowfoot dancing with Shirley Temple up the stairs and off camera.

"Hey, did you hear about what happened with Viper Bugloss?"

"You mean that guy that steals stuff out of campgrounds? I've never seen him, but I've heard tell. You mean that guy?"

"Yeah, that guy. I heard he got arrested at a pow wow for paying kids to sell his crazy statues. He was paying them with apple jack. What do you think of that?"

"Wow, that's quite a story."

"Sure is. Makes you think, doesn't it?"

"Maybe. Makes you think about what?"

"I don't know, just makes you think."

> Yard Sale: Owner in Jail
> All must go!!!
> Carvings $25
> Apple Jack $0

LITTLE SPOKANE RIVER KOAN #1

A Noxious Weed Board volunteer walked below Sellheim Springs. He pulled up Spotted Knapweed, Toadflax, and Musk Thistle as he went. He was disgusted by the way so many invasive plants had been carelessly introduced. No wonder this was no longer pastureland for dairy cows.

He stopped by a pool where Mister White lay in the shade of a black walnut tree.

He turned around, walked upstream, threw the plants in the current, and headed for his car.

DREAM FISHING
THE LITTLE SPOKANE
LIBRARY

I recall finding the Dream Fishing the Little
Spokane Library on a late summer morning. I
was taking a tour of cemeteries dotting the
Little Spokane landscape. All of these
cemeteries are off the beaten path. Some are
cared for by individuals with singular
missions. Some are cared for by time itself.
   The way to the Dream Fishing the Little
Spokane Library passes through roundabouts and
under stop lights. I drove past a gas and
convenience store, by an evangelical church's
expansive parking lot, and then down to the
Little Spokane River. A sign along the way
warns:

NO TRESPASSING

VIOLATORS WILL BE PROSECUTED

TO THE FULL EXTENT OF THE LAW

   I crossed over a bridge. Everything around
here is a bridge. Some bridges are of steel
and concrete, and others are of wood. Some
bridges are simply points from here to there,
ancient, fords where feet have followed other
feet. On this late summer morning this bridge
was the fresh white of newly laid concrete.
This bridge smiled the smile of wedding vows
gone by. "Now I pronounce you man and wife."

16

"Now I lay me down to sleep." "I pledge
allegiance to the flag."

Turning off the off-the-beaten path I came
upon a cemetery. The grounds were surrounded
by a pine board fence. A zinc galvanized gate
had no padlock or chain. I pushed open the
gate and walked inside. The grounds were not
mowed or watered. Weathered ponderosa pine
shaded the native bunch grass and dogbane.
Weathered tombstones stood here and there,
behind this tree and on that rise. The graves
were old Polaroids stored in a Buster Brown
shoe box and slipped under a bed. The mattress
sagged from years of old-woman sleep.

"Beware God's Angels ARE HERE"

"Infant Riley Twins"

"Blusom"

A yellow, lichen-covered, plastic chair,
broken

"Mattie Jackman 1867-1922"

"Infant Owens"

"Baby Buster"

Marbles embedded in concrete

"Lawrence Blar 1903"

"Infant Fletcher"

Next I walked between two pines and into
the Dream Fishing the Little Spokane Library.
Wisdom placed the circulation desk at the
center and made every patron a librarian. The
Dewey Decimal or Library of Congress systems
are not used. No one arranges the volumes in

17

any way. In fact, the shelves of the Dream Fishing the Little Spokane Library are empty.

Like I said, I was taking a tour of cemeteries. I recall standing in the Dream Fishing the Little Spokane Library and being in one of my many moods. I was thinking about America's children, the way they leave their morning homes, sleepy eyed, their breath fogging the frostbite air. I thought about the dirty yellow bus coming down the street trailing its carbon monoxide exhaust. "Hey, what d'y'think we're go'n t'do in school today?" "Fuck you, I don' know. My Dad got drunk again and hit my mom a bunch of times." "That sucks. My dad left before I was born. He lives in California. My mom says he sells meth."

I was working at being a school teacher, which wasn't going the way I'd liked. Oh, I looked forward to seeing kids every day. They always brought me smiles or fell asleep in class. I didn't care much which one. What I'd never liked was the smell, that desks-in-rows, wrong answer, threat-behind-the-curtain smell. Maybe you remember America's 1960's white knight, the way he blasted dirt away with his laundry detergent lance. I objected to that.

So, like I said, I was thinking about America's children, and now I was in the middle of my first visit to the Dream Fishing the Little Spokane Library. The sunlight had a gentleness in the way it was filtered by the pine needles. Words came to me as if I had reached for a volume from one of the shelves, but, of course, I hadn't because the library shelves were empty.

> Finally the jailer came, opened
> the cell door and took her out.
> She remained a long time, and when
> she returned I gathered from the
> whispered conversation with the

older one, the following: That he
had taken her down to see a man on
the floor below—a sweetheart, she
called him to me afterward. She
went again and remained a long
time, and whispering told the
other woman on her return that
"Bert" (I judged to be the jailer)
would have brought "Jack" up but
for this woman, indicating me.
"They don't trust her," she said.[1]

I held these words in my mind for a while. I
turned them the way I'd turn one of those sea
shells, the ones that echo the ocean's voice,
deep, and no way not to imagine being drowned.
    Then I heard a breeze up in the tree
limbs. The breeze came down, tousling my hair.
More words came to me.

I regret extremely to have to
state, that Kootamey [sic] is now
no more. He received an injury, in
falling off a horse, when last
among his friends; the effects of
which he seems never to have
recovered. He died on Easter
Monday, at my house, after a
gradual and almost painless ebbing
of Nature's powers. During the
early stages of his malady, he was
painfully silent and reserved on
the subject of his spiritual
welfare; ... Mr. Smith asked him
in my hearing, "Kootamey, do you
pray?" He said faintly, "Yes,
Sir." Mr. Smith rejoined: "And
what do you pray for?" With a look
of deep concern, he answered, "I
pray to God to pardon my sins, and
wash my soul."[2]

I turned these words the way I'd turn a gem stone, not a cut and polished one, but a raw, right-from-the-earth stone, the sort of stone from which jewelers remove so-called imperfections and impurities.

At this moment a red squirrel commenced to give me notice. Its chatter brought to mind the Walden Pond words of Henry David Thoreau, "[the chickaree] kept up the queerest chuckling and chirruping and vocal pirouetting and gurgling sounds that ever were heard; ... and fell into a strain of invective that was irresistible." More words then followed, though these words in no way were about squirrels.

> being Sunday the medicine chief
> had devotional exercises with his
> followers   he formed them into a
> ring men women and children and
> after an address they danced to a
> tune in dancing the[y] keep the
> feet in the same position the
> whole time mer[e]ly jumping up to
> the tune keeping the hands in
> front of them at intervals he
> addressed them.[3]

I stopped to gaze upon these words. I walked about them as if I had come upon a horse hide spread upon a tree, a grave marker, a sign of respect for what had once been.

And just like that it started to rain. I knew it was time to leave the Dream Fishing the Little Spokane Library. It doesn't rain much here on late summer mornings. As I said, I was thinking about America's children. The children were probably home texting their friends or out fishing at summer camp. Maybe one had just pulled a pumpkinseed sunfish off the dock on Fan Lake, a tributary on the West Branch of the Little Spokane, and that

kid was heard to say, "Hey, look, I got a
fish. What kind o'fish d'y'think this is?"

FOOTNOTES

TO THE DREAM FISHING

THE LITTLE SPOKANE LIBRARY

CHAPTER

I was thinking you might like some explanation for what's in the "Dream Fishing the Little Spokane Library" chapter. You might have the impression that we writers sometimes get a bit carried away. We think we're Salvadore Dali's melting clocks or Mina Loy's "Delirious Avenues/lit/with the chandelier souls/of infusoria/from Pharoah's tombstones//lead/to mercurial doomsdays." Sometimes we get just a bit too precious. Fair enough.

It might help to know that taking long walks along the Little Spokane River can lead to such things. Oh, sure, there are mosquito swarms in the summer and ice to fall through in the winter, but sometimes a mind gets a chance to get off the tracks. Think of Dream Fishing as a train wreck or a library or even a visit with Carl Jung. Think of Dream Fishing as something in a child's hand.

And if you've come this far and you're not persuaded when your boyfriend tells you this sort of thing is great, and if only you could feel what he is feeling and only if the zipper on your Daisy Dukes would drop to its knees, you might want some help with what is in the "Dream Fishing the Little Spokane Library" chapter.

You might be having trouble with, [1]"Finally the jailer came, opened the cell door and took her out. ..." and so on.

These words were written by Elizabeth Gurley Flynn and published in the *Industrial Worker*, v 1, n 39, 15 December 1909.

Mrs. Flynn writes about her arrest during the mostly forgotten Spokane Free Speech Fight of 1909-1910. The problem was that Spokane had twenty-one employment agencies up and down Stevens Street. Down-and-outs paid $1.00 to get a job cutting timber or digging mine shafts. They went to work for a day or two and then were fired. As a result these out-of-work timberbeasts and miners crawled back to Spokane and scratched up another $1.00 for another job.

Not surprisingly Spokane's down-and-outs became increasingly angry. In response the Spokane City Council outlawed public speaking for anyone but the Salvation Army. Publicly describing conditions suddenly became dangerous, which suited Elizabeth Gurley Flynn just fine. She came to town and became editor of the *Industrial Worker*. The previous editors had all been arrested. Soon enough the pregnant Flynn was arrested too and thrown into jail. While locked up she witnessed a fellow cellmate pimped out as a prostitute.

"Hey, where did they take you?" "Down to see a sweetheart." "Is that what they call it?" "Yeah, when *you*'re in here. Now, I'm go'n t'turn the light down so y'can rest."

You also might be having trouble with, [2]"I regret extremely to have to state, that Kootamey [sic] is now no more. ..." and so on. These words were written by the Reverend D. T. Jones and published in "Church Missionary Papers," v LXX, Midsummer 1833 and collected in *Missionary papers [afterw.], Church missionary paper [afterw.] Quarterly church missionary paper [afterw.]C.M.S. quarterly paper*. 1841.

The Reverend D. T. Jones writes about Kootenay's death after he was thrown from a horse. Jones is worried about the state of Kootenay's soul because Kootenay was born to people now known as the Kootenai tribe. At first, Kootenay didn't talk, which was a sure sign to Jones that the boy's soul was destined to suffer the fate of all savage souls. Then, after some prompting, Kootenay offered the correct catechismal response. Jones was relieved. Kootenay's words and death allowed Jones to experience the full fruit of the white man's burden. Jones could rest in the knowledge that he was a faithful instrument of God and gave Kootenay a chance at salvation.

Interestingly enough most of us in and around Spokane don't know about Kootaney, but we do know about his friend, Spokane Garry. History tells us that both boys were sent off together by their fathers to the North-West American Mission on the Red River over a thousand miles away. Both boys were renamed for two officials of the Hudson's Bay Company, Nicholas Garry and Robert Pelly, and both boys learned to speak English and French and to read The Bible. One boy came home to be called Chief Spokane Garry by Europeans and his own people, to found the first-ever school in the Spokane area, to struggle to keep the peace during the Steptoe-Wright War, and to be driven off his farm, his house destroyed. Today a middle school, park, and monument have been dedicated to him. The other boy was thrown from a horse and died on alien soil. He served as an anecdote for an Anglican homily. Only God knows about the state of Kootenay Pelly's soul. If you listen carefully, he might be heard to say, "Garry, I've a feeling we're not in the land of the coyote anymore."

Finally you might be having trouble with, [3]"[the medicine chief] formed them into a ring men women and children and after an address they danced to a tune ..." and so on. These words were written by entrepreneur, explorer and amateur ethnographer Nathaniel J. Wyeth and were published in *The Correspondence and Journals of Captain Nathaniel J. Wyeth, 1831-6*. University Press, 1899.

Captain Wyeth is writing about the dancing of Salish and Nez Percè peoples. Inland Northwest Native people along the Spokane danced for the sun, the buffalo, scalps, animal guardians, among other things. They also danced as a way to hold themselves together as their friends, relatives, and culture dissolved away. Wyeth is describing this later sort of dancing. The problem started when the smallpox epidemic of 1782 killed half the local population. So many people died that dogs ate some of the bodies. Mount St. Helens then erupted, sending apocalyptic ash across the Little Spokane. Next came white traders and trappers bearing new technology, new ideas, and new diseases. Inland Northwest Native women along the Spokane went off with too many European men and were discarded like empty whiskey bottles.

The dancing Wyeth described is often categorized as messianic by Christianized people. This dancing has been variously called the prophet, spirit, dream, feather, or ghost dance. An important distinction must be made; these dancers never went to dancing school. These dancers never thought to write down how their movements were to be done. The Anglicans at the North-West American Mission gave Spokane Garry a *Book of Common Prayer* but not Thomas Wilson's *The quadrille and cotillion panorama*. All that you can be sure of is that this sort of dancing disappeared from the

Little Spokane area soon after Wyeth wrote his description.

"Hey, did y'just get back from y'r walk? Looks like y'r feelin' down? Why don't y'get up and stick y'r hands out in front. I'll start up this music. Let's try a little Jim Boyd. 'Inchelium' should get us hoppin'." "Thanks." "You bet."

SPOKANE DEATH SENTENCE

Mary Walker's diary May 25, 1839.

> No worship in the morn with the
> Indians on account of a dog have broken
> into the house in the night. They talk
> rather bad but finally said they had
> killed the dog so all goes on right
> again.

DREAM FISHING

THE LITTLE SPOKANE

GOES TO SCHOOL

I went to school with Dream Fishing the Little Spokane. I was in the ninth grade. Dream Fishing the Little Spokane sat right in front of me. He was new to my school, and hence new to me, but like so many of us kids back in those days, we were having a lot of trouble with the idea of school.

Our teacher, who was in his first year of wrangling America's youth, had gone to college to avoid the fate of U. S. soldiers in Vietnam. He did not want to be shot to pieces, soaked in Agent Orange, or blown to smithereens; you get the picture. Instead, he signed up to embrace the fate of U. S. teachers in America's classrooms.

Early in September our teacher was directed to use a grammar book. He told us kids the book was about something called transformational-generative grammar, the latest thing, and he was supposed to teach us all about it. He did not teach us that transformational-generative grammar was a psychological construct meant to be a shotgun wedding between cognitive psychology and English grammar, a wedding arranged by one Mr. Noam Chomsky. Our teacher also did not tell us that Noam Chomsky was on President Nixon's "Enemies List." Chomsky was a busy man and did not want our teacher to embrace the fate of U. S. soldiers in Vietnam.

As we were soon to find out, our teacher was having trouble with the idea of Chomsky's grammar book. We watched as our teacher did something unexpected with that grammar book. He started by carrying the book over to the classroom windows. They were the sort of windows built into a lot of 1950's and '60's structures. The windows had extruded steel frames. The glass stayed in place without the glazing. They were crafted without the direct aid of human hands. The windows whispered of a future where leisure was plentiful, no one got sick, and space travel was commonplace.

We then watched as our teacher finished what we thought was so unexpected. He thrust the book out the window and dropped it. The book travelled past similar windows built into the principal's office. Our classroom was one story up, and that transformational-generative grammar book, an atomic grammar device pointing to the future, fell like Little Boy over Hiroshima. The impact tumbled the walls of our minds, and the heat melted the skins of our souls. Our teacher was also having a lot of trouble with the idea of school.

After our school day's final bell, Dream Fishing the Little Spokane and I walked home together. He told me he first went to school on April 12, 1825. He said that before that day, children learned by listening, watching, and doing. Kids learned by learning. People lived by living.

I asked Dream Fishing the Little Spokane what it was like to go to school for the first time back in 1825.

He said it all started when these guys named David Thompson and Jaco Finlay came around. These guys cut down trees and built log houses and other structures. They said they wanted everybody to do less root gathering, horse racing, and fishing. They said they wanted more animal hunting. They only wanted the skins.

David Thompson and Jaco Finlay said, "To hell with all the other stuff."

Dream Fishing the Little Spokane's dad said these guys didn't even care about beaver teeth. They didn't care that beaver teeth are good for making tools and jewelry, and they didn't care that the old guys taught the young guys to gamble by tossing beaver teeth. "Hey, look what I got in the trunk of my car." "Shit, man, I got t'have some of that. What's it go'n t'cost me?" "Just a bit of a lifestyle change, and I'll throw in this bag of unintended consequences 'cuz we're friends."

Then Dream Fishing the Little Spokane said this guy named Mr. George Simpson showed up. Simpson told his dad that Dream Fishing the Little Spokane should go to Simpson's school.

His dad said, "Son, if you go far away to this school, when you come back, you will be one of them."

"But, Dad, I don't want to go away to a strange place with strange people. I want to stay here with you."

"I know, Son, but I think this can be good for everyone. I don't want you to leave, but right now there isn't much reason for a young man to stay here."

Dream Fishing the Little Spokane said he walked over a thousand miles. He walked and rode in wagons. He paddled boats. He said he thought when he was little, going root digging was a long walk, and when he was older, going to see his cousins on Flathead Lake was a much longer walk.

"Where are we, now?"

"The Red River School in Manitoba."

"Where's Manitoba?"

"It's beyond the mountains where the sun rises."

"What's the Red River School?"

"It's a place where you'll learn to read the Word of God. You will learn to plant potatoes, pumpkins, and squash. You will also learn to grow and harvest wheat and corn."

At this point in his story, Dream Fishing the Little Spokane and I stood in front of my house. It was a working family special, built in the 1950s, a little wood frame box standing like an American stockade. World War II had ended, and the melting pot mix of survivors, having pledged their fealty every morning in school, claimed their share of the spoils through America's G.I. Bill. Little wooden stockades lined the streets in every direction, an Inland Empire in every home.

I said goodbye to my friend and left him to go inside. I didn't know where Dream Fishing the Little Spokane lived, but I knew it wasn't in my neighborhood. I hoped his home wasn't much further.

He didn't come to school the next day. The seat in front of me stayed empty for a day, then a second, soon a week went by, and later the weeks turned into months. To the best of my knowledge, Dream Fishing the Little Spokane never came back to school. I guess he decided he had better things to do.

ANXIETY COMES

TO THE HOUSE ON THOR

Anxiety came to the house on Thor March 16,
1939. Hitler and his Nazi machine entered
Czechoslovakia. The Shah of Iran married
Princess Fawzia of Egypt. And Hungary annexed
the republic of Karpato-Ukraine. It wasn't a
good year for an anxious, two-bedroom bungalow
to be born.

   The street had been named for the Norse
god Thor. Nobody seems to know why. Somebody
named the next street east after the Norse
goddess Freya. One wonders if the naming was
subversive. After all, Thor's hammer was a bit
of agitprop graffiti carved to resist
Christian incursions. "Wan'o confess and
flagellate?" "Not really." "Oh."

   It should also be noted that Thor was a
cross-dresser. The story goes that a thief
stole Thor's hammer and buried it deep in the
earth. The thief told Thor that he would tell
him where he hid the hammer if, in exchange,
the thief married Freya. Not surprisingly
Freya said, "Yeah, you and whose army?"
Instead Thor's buddy Loki suggested that Thor
deck himself out as the bride. Thor was good
with Loki's plan, and one cross-dressing
episode later, Thor got his hammer back.

   Much later the house on Thor found itself
up for sale. In the spring of 2014, many
questions swirled about. Who would purchase
the house? A slum lord? An urban homesteader?
A low-level dope dealer intent on supporting

his habit? A night watchman whose afternoons were spent fly fishing the upper Spokane? "Wonder if the caddis fly hatch is on? Think I'll take my rod down to the banks and check it out. I can throw in a few tweaker twitches in the slack water. Might hook an old-timey, cadmium-infused cutthroat. Get out my well-seasoned, iron skillet and fry it up with bacon and onions."

As it turned out, it was none of these who bought the house on Thor. Instead, the buyer was a worry-filled young man. His name was Colby, and he was a bit desperate for a place to live. His lease was up. He needed a place to safely lay him down to sleep. There was always a cardboard box underneath the Monroe Street Bridge, but he wasn't a sucker for such Romantic visions. He'd been cold enough to have nightmares about death from exposure. He had no interest in becoming the stuff from which hypothermic obituaries are written.

Colby had never done very well in school. Some of his teachers thought he was difficult. The word defiant was bandied about. The word lazy didn't follow too far behind. He preferred to retreat to his bedroom and marry electronic parts. There was peace in the combining of transistors, regulators, and resistors. He and the solder would melt and flow as one. There was nothing difficult about electronics.

Relatives told Colby his high school days were the best days of his life. He sure hoped not. And life after high school didn't start out much better. He tried his hand at college. In fact he tried for five years. He tried so hard he thought about buying a gun. Pulling the trigger had to be difficult, but not as difficult as getting up the next day and going to college.

Then one day he picked up the newspaper. He looked over the headlines. "Cheating, a

Normal Stage in Child's Development."
"Scenario Bleak for NFL Players in Overtuned
Boat." "'Comb Over' Comment Gets Juror Tossed
from Trial." Toward the back he found the
"Jobs" section. Skimming his finger down the
page, he stopped and read.

> I am looking for someone to help
> me out. I have a sushi business
> and right now we are making some
> big orders. What happens is there
> is often a lot of leftover rice
> and seafood odds and ends. We
> usually end up with a pile of food
> we don't want to throw away. If
> you love seafood and rice and want
> to get paid to eat all the
> leftover tuna and octopus that you
> can, then come work for us. This
> position is perfect for somebody
> who eats a lot and is hungry all
> the time. Because it's seafood and
> steamed rice, you won't even get
> fat. If you are interested, text
> me about why you love sushi so
> much. Right now we'd only need you
> a couple of days a week. It's hard
> to say how much longer beyond this
> month the job will last. Who
> knows, we might need you
> permanently!

Anything with free food sounded good, but
Colby wasn't really into raw fish. Moving down
the page Colby stopped at this one.

> My wife is in jail, and chances
> are she's not getting out anytime
> soon. She stabbed this woman in a
> bar when the bitch bought a whole
> round of drinks and charged them
> to her. The bitch died of

peritonitis, so there's not much
chance she's getting out soon. The
deal is she's got this real
hankering for conjugal visits, if
you know what I mean? I really
need you to keep her happy because
it's her disability that I'm
living off of. I don't have the
stamina to visit her all the time
and make her see the Aurora
Borealis. I need you to visit her
regular, so she don't file for
divorce. I will pay you $25 a
visit as long as you keep her
happy.

"Wow," Colby thought, "takes all kinds.
Twenty-five dollars is twenty-five dollars,
but this seems to be the fire without the
frying pan." Better to keep his finger going
down the page.

Got some experience in electronics
repair? Want to keep airplanes in
the air instead of falling from
the sky? Like your own work bench
where nobody will bother you? Give
us a call, and if we like you, and
you like us, we'll work something
out.

Now this was more like it.
Just like that Colby gave those folks a
call, applied, interviewed, and took a
homegrown electronics test. They liked him. He
liked them. He stopped going to college and
took the job. He never bought that gun.
As a result he began to save up money. He
didn't have a car. He didn't eat for any
pleasure except to stave off hunger. He made
pilgrimages to the dark corners of local
grocery outlets. Label-less cans lay in

bargain bins like day-old bums sleeping off bottles of Night Train. In this grocery religion, he found sustenance at the mission of the damaged and discarded.

With the money he saved, he avoided that cardboard box beneath the Monroe Street Bridge. Not one to turn down a handout, he got in on the CityLift Program, "To support sustainable homeownership and advance neighborhood stability." Colby had developed radar for the too-good-to-be-true. He'd seen that piece of fresh meat just lying out for the taking. THWACK, and the steel jaws snapped his tibia like a twig underfoot.

All the same he didn't look a gift horse in the mouth. He asked questions. He found that the CityLift Program was fallout from the financial meltdown of 2008. Colby decided to be a raccoon who has come down to the stream. He decided to turn over every rock until he came to the house on Thor on March 16, 2014.

Colby's decision gave the house on Thor hope that it would find its happy ending. It wished Colby might turn out to be mother's little helper. It wished to live in its own Spokane Valley of the Dolls.

But the house on Thor needed more than Rock Candy Mountain and Pie in Sky. It needed some reassurance from Sister Ylva who lived right up the street. Sister Ylva read palms and tarot cards. Tea leaves spoke to her. Visions of the future and voices from those departed populated her ripe spirit full to bursting. This was the perfect time for the house on Thor to pay her a visit.

What the house on Thor heard wasn't promising. It wasn't the sort of karmic payback it wanted for all these lean years. After the reading the house on Thor posted this review on Google:

Boy, that was a buzz kill. Ylva brewed up some tea, and we looked at the leaves. She also dusted off her crystal ball. All I learned was that my life sucks. She told me, "Your life is full of broken promises and empty dreams." You got to be kidding me, Eminem lyrics? Then she tried to sell me this sage bundle. I suppose it might smell good, but I got sage in my cupboard. Then she told me she couldn't turn all this around in one visit. She said that if my life was going to get any better, I needed to come back a lot. What the hell, I don't have that kind of money. I'll figure out how to recharge my own spiritual battery. I have no idea why anyone would go here. I'm pretty pissed at myself for not being more DIY. You don't need this anymore than I do!

Although Colby bought the house on Thor, things began to unravel when Colby heard a heroin treatment center was going in a few blocks down. It wasn't like he didn't have sympathy for addicts. His life hadn't always been a picnic. Everybody deserves a chance to pull themselves out of the shit hole they're sitting in. "Hey buddy, can you give me a hand?" "Your hand's all shitty. I don't think so." "Oh, sorry."

But things had changed since Colby had bought the house on Thor. He met this girl. Her name was Clarice. She smelled really nice. She smelled of the mock-orange that grew by the railroad tracks of his childhood. When he was a kid, he used to go down there in late spring. He'd sit on a rail and let the orange-filled breeze come to him. Sometimes the sun would warm the railroad ties like convenience store hot dogs. Piquant orange would mix with mordant creosote. On days like these the fragrance reminded him of his mother's cleaning product. When she scrubbed the toilet, she complained, "What the hell do you people do in here! Colby, go get a shovel. You're go'n t'dig an outhouse out back. I'm not go'n t'touch this thing ever again!"

Fortunately mock-orange Clarice did not remind him of his mother. Clarice was much too practical. She wanted a world that tended toward emotional security and physical safety. And she liked Colby more than his mother. Clarice was elderberries. Colby's mother was water hemlock. "STOP. Water hemlocks are the most poisonous plants in North America. All parts are deadly poisonous. Even a small mouthful can kill an adult."

"Colby, I hear they're putting in a heroin recovery center down on Thor. Don't you think that could really hurt property values around here?" Clarice said.

"I suppose."

"Don't you think you might want to sell this house? You said you were desperate when you bought it. I don't want you to lose money on your investment."

"I guess you're right."

What the house on Thor smelled wasn't promising. The smell made it anxious. For some reason it reminded the house on Thor of Panzer tank exhaust in 1939.

THE CRYSTAL PALACE
SLAVE SHIP

On 1950's summer mornings Donny popped from
his bed like a bottle cap from a Mae West,
ten-ounce, orange pop bottle. He was a
great white hunter in the mold of Alan
Black and Frederick Selous. Summer was for
travelling into the Wandermere Wasteland's
heart of darkness just above the wilds of
the Little Spokane River.

Atop Donny's painted-blue, pine dresser
lay his glass jar collection.

4 grape jelly jars, 12 oz

3 peanut butter jars, 18 oz

1 Spanish olive jar, 7 3/4 oz

1 "Inland Empire Pickle" jar, 1 qt

Each jar's emptiness exhilarated Donny the
same way trespassing construction sites at
sundown exhilarated him. He liked to walk 2 X
4 gangways onto fresh plywood and stop between
newly raised studs. He liked to stand where
the basement fell away, empty, into darkness.
In the evening of 1950's housing developments,
the future was clear, a pyramid for every
American, an egalitarian land of the dead.

Donny had used his mom's can opener to
punch six to ten holes in each jar lid. He
often watched his mom use this tool to release
chicken noodle soup and pork and beans. He was

aware that he lived in a magical time. His mom's *Ladies Home Journal*, September 1952, told wondrous stories.

Ah! Magic Aroma ...

This coffee pot went to college!

You'll get compliments every day
for coffee made the WearEver way.
Why? Because every WearEver coffee
maker incorporates the results of
exhaustive research by a great
American university to determine
the exact coffee pot construction
to give you perfect coffee every
time!

Neither Donny's mom nor dad had been to college, but their coffee pot had. No doubt life was getting better all the time.

Donny's dad got on a twelve hour shift at the local aluminum reduction plant. The factory was built when Donny's dad was a kid. Back then it made aluminum for B-17 Flying Fortress bombers and P-51 Mustang fighters. Aluminum had lightened the load for the heavy business of war. Ten years later Donny's dad was hired on as a carbon anode loader/unloader. He kept the electricity flowing through the nine-hundred-and-fifty degree aluminum oxide and made sure the fluoride, carbon monoxide, and carbon dioxide bubbled to the top. The war was over now, most assuredly, temporarily, and aluminum continued to lighten the load, this time for the heavy business of business.

Soon enough Donny's dad was on his way, and, as a result, Donny's mom made him an honest man. The marriage was sure as a Formica-topped, kitchen table in a Sears' storefront window. And just as sure Donny's

40

mom and dad kept an appointment at Spokane's First National Bank. There, inside the bank's polished, black and red granite slabs, they signed onto the American Dream. There, as they looked through the aluminum-framed, glass panels, Donny's dad traded thirty years of his life for a piece of the Devil's Triangle.

No one was quite sure why Donny's neighborhood was called the Devil's Triangle. It was bounded by the Y inside Highways 2 and 395 and built for war-effort workers at the local aluminum reduction plant. The name Devil's Triangle didn't have the same ring as neighboring Lidgerwood and Country Homes. The name wasn't modern. It came out of Spokane's not-so-distant past: ghost-brothels like the Colonial Hotel, specter-saloons like Durkin's Whiskies Wines Cigars, and banshee-revolts like the Dynamite Express.

Donny grabbed "The Inland Empire Pickle" jar from his pine dresser and flew from the Devil's Triangle on his twenty-six inch, defense model Schwinn. His family couldn't afford to buy Donny a 1950's Schwinn Hornet and certainly not the stream-lined, chrome-plated, cantilevered-forked Phantom. Even a used 1930's Aerocycle was out of the question. On the day his new-to-him bike rolled up the front walk, his dad said, "Donny, take care of your tools, and they'll take care of you." During the evenings Donny studied his dad working on his IEL Beaver chainsaw. Like his dad, Donny became a minister of bearings and a pastor of chains.

Donny didn't know "The Inland Empire Pickle" jar was soon to be a crystal palace slave ship. How does anyone know such things? It's like just before a hotel gets torn down. Every day you drive past that corner, the one where the hotel stands like Lady Liberty's torch, the patrons registering, the fine print saying, "Give me your tired, your poor, your huddled masses ..." You never expect on that

particular day that something will be
different, something will be wrong. You drive
past, and the shadow of the hotel is gone. The
pillars, the façade, the windows, and the
signage are gone. The tired patrons no longer
huddle inside. It's just like that thing she
could have said, that thing she always said
before, but now she didn't say it this time,
and nothing will ever be the same.

Once Donny entered the shrub steppe and
black pine of the Wandermere Wasteland, one
thing led to another as it always does, most
assuredly, temporarily. Donny looked up to see
a boy standing above him. He recognized the
boy from his elementary school. The boy's name
was Richard. They had been in same classroom
for the last few years but had never sat next
to one another. Awhile back Donny had gotten
in trouble for passing Richard an answer to a
test question, "What were Aztec sacrificial
knives made of?"

"Hard stuff," Donny wrote on a corner torn
from his test paper. He remembered letting go
of the answer into Richard's hand, a message
in a bottle released into the current of this
creek or that river.

Donny knew Richard did not live in the
Devil's Triangle; instead, Richard lived
beyond the Wandermere Wasteland along the
floodplain of the Little Spokane. The shack
where Richard lived had automobile carcasses
in various states of decomposition stopped
over here and in this place among the
serviceberry and cottonwood,

"Hey, what you doin'?"

"Huntin' grasshoppers."

"Puttin' 'em in that jar, huh? I got an
idea," and Richard jumped down. His shadow
trailed behind like Death's robe, tattered
from eons of weary use. His outstretched hand,
strong, caught hold of "The Inland Empire
Pickle" jar.

"See, we're go'n t'take this jar and fill it with grasshoppers. I'll help." Richard pulled "The Inland Empire Pickle" jar free from Donny's grasp.

Donny had already captured three mature grasshoppers. He had been planning to return home, to give them some lawn-fresh grass and plum tree leaves to munch. He had been planning to keep them under the north eave of his house so that they would be shaded enough to avoid certain heat stroke. He dreamed of curating a modern zoo like Stamford Raffles of London's Regents Park. He thought himself the King Solomon of the Devil's Triangle.

Richard had other ideas. He filled "The Inland Empire Pickle" jar with grasshoppers. The jar was packed tight as rush hour mass transit. One insect writhed against the other in their crystal palace slave ship, working for some unavailable space, some unobtainable comfort. The scene was Andy Warhol's homage to Hieronymus Bosch.

"Okay, I think that's good enough. Cool isn't it? Bet you never thought I could catch this many!

"So, now let's have some real fun. We're havin' fun right? Bet y'never thought you're go'n t'have this much fun when y'got up this morning, did ya? I really know how t'have a good time, don't I?"

"Sure."

Richard led, and Donny followed. It was one those situations where better intentions are bulldozed beneath a psychopathic destiny. The cattle cars leave the Polish ghetto at 1:00 PM. Gravity pulls Big Boy homeward bound.

Richard stopped in front of a 1951 Kaiser Dragon with a scarlet, padded vinyl roof. This car had embodied someone's dream. Once driven from the showroom, this car became both fetish and altar. Now this car was trash left on the Wandermere Wasteland between the Little

Spokane River and the Devil's Triangle. This car was a shipwrecked pioneer's wagon, broken, a bleached and shattered horse skull.

"Off comes the top and over they go on t'the roof." Richard stepped back and admired his handiwork. His smile spread like a black cold front blowing out of Canada.

For a moment the grasshoppers struggled to find their equilibrium. Gravity's pull was wrong. Pressure from wriggling flesh made it difficult to establish equilibrium. After a minute or so the mass settled. The wait for what came next was awful.

Soon enough the sun took affect inside "The Inland Empire Pickle" jar. Slowly, inexorably, the temperature inside the glass rose. Donny and Richard watched each grasshopper push against the others in a desperate effort to lower its body temperature. An extended family of polar bears all on the last chunk of pack ice, there was the jitterbug of death in a pressure cooker, and then a fox trot, and then no more.

"Wow, that was great!" Richard said marveling at his effect on the world. "Wasn't that great?"

"Yeah, great." Donny felt sick in the way he felt sick seeing maggots fall off a road kill, hit three days ago, guts ripped and spilled like luggage torn open by a baggage conveyor, nothing to be done, the pearly white fly fetuses packed like cars under a burger joint sign.

"So, let's pop it off and see what we've got. You're go'n t'love it. Here we go!"

Richard lifted "The Inland Empire Pickle" jar, but packed tightly and cooked in place, most of the grasshopper corpses stayed put. Only a few, stiff-legged and soft-bellied, tumbled out.

"Donny, come here and look. This is really neat."

44

On closer inspection Donny saw that the glass oven had melted the Red Dragon's vinyl roof. As the vinyl cooled, a few bodies had become partially entombed. Legs, antennae, and single eyes stood like petrified tree trunks thrust from badlands' sediment.

"Jesus, Mary, and Joseph Z. Christ, that's the best one of these I ever done. Ain't that somethin'. Whooo-eee, when y'come with me, y'never know what's go'n t'happen. Ain't that right? Hey, Donny, where'd y'go?"

Donny didn't stay to marvel over their handiwork. He left "The Inland Empire Pickle" jar behind and rode his defense model Schwinn up out of the Wandermere Wasteland. He feverishly pedaled in the direction of an American flag flying above the Devil's Triangle.

* * *

A local newspaper reported that *a housewife has disappeared from her home in North Spokane. Her husband, an employee of the aluminum reduction plant, and their son, age twelve, have been able to offer no explanation about her whereabouts.*

* * *

After Donny returned home from the Wandermere Wasteland, very little seemed out of the ordinary except for a can opener stuck in the kitchen wall and the kitchen door left wide open. Donny never forgot the way the aluminum screen door banged to and fro in the summer afternoon breeze.

WANDERMERE SKI JUMP

"Elvrum Takes Off," *Spokesman Review*,
22 January 1964.

Fighting the crosswinds that even
the aviators took note of yesterday,
winds that flipped aloft the slats of
many less agile jumpers, the Cascade Ski
Club star John Elvrum sailed 120 feet on
his first takeoff.

THE GREAT NORTHERN TRAIN WRECK

> "As to recklessness, anyone who knew Munson and appreciated the fact that he had for years traveled that very track, will not suggest it." (*Spokane Press*, 24 July 1906)

Finley liked to fish for tench. Like him tench were transplants. Like him they ate whatever was available. Here in the Chain Lakes just east of the ghost town of Camden, Washington, tench mucked close to shore for insect larvae and little invertebrates. Unlike tench, Finley mucked in the morning for last night's hamburger gravy and some other day's peas. Dumpster diving is the most American of all pastimes, right after closing time, right outside a five-star restaurant.

Finley couldn't dodge the fact that he was a foster child. He knew he was just one bad report away from moving again. He'd heard it all before, "Yes, yes, we'll take him in. Our house isn't a home unless there's a kid around. Y'know, ma'am, we just want to make a difference in the world. It's a shame what happens with some of these kids. We really appreciate you givin' us a chance to help a kid down on his luck. We been there, y'know?"

Finley knew not to fall for the sweet talk adults made. They always spoke as if he were not in the room. He wasn't asked about where he was going to live and who he was going to live with. He did know that he was worth more than $703.00 a month. That's how much "Level One" foster kids were worth. He was what those in the foster system called a "Level Two." He knew he was presently worth $880.92 a month. He made his foster parents an extra $77.92 because he was more than 3 hours of trouble a week. He was a blue light special, a buyer-beware item in America's bargain bin.

A few foster homes back, Finley got left in the car. His foster Mom had an itch to scratch and needed to travel light. Left alone, he mucked about the car to find something, anything, amusing. Finley had a raven's eye. Most things could be a diamond if a facet caught the light. On this windows-not-cracked afternoon, he punched in the cigarette lighter. It was amusing to look at the glowing coil and watch the orange turn to a heat-stressed gray. He reinserted the lighter, pulled it again, and then put the fire-of-hell end to his forearm. After what seemed like a half minute or so, he took the lighter away from his arm and studied his red, beginning-to-blister, skin. He did it over and over until he had created an extensive mosaic. He was surprised it did not hurt like he thought. Oh, it hurt alright, just not as much as he thought.

Tench fishing was best done on a summer Sunday when waking up was like opening a fresh box of Honey Hits. Summer Sunday mornings had a nutritional value like no other.

"Suzie, please pass me the Honey Hits. It's the number one cereal in America because it has 15 grams of sugar in a 27 gram serving. That's 55.6% sugar by weight. It's like rocket fuel and why kids from Finland to Australia want to be American just like you and me."

But on this particular Sunday morning there was no box of Honey Hits in the house. Instead the adults were sleeping off Saturday night. School was a fading bad dream. And the sun came up like a Digger gold piece saying, "WITHIN A FREE FRAME OF REFERENCE ... THE FREE MEN OF THE WHOLE WORLD (NOT TO BE CONSTRUED TO BE REAL IN ANY AMERICAN SENSE)."

Freedom on a Sunday morning was fishing, and Finley was a true fisherman, which is to say his gear was a collection of sacred objects. Finley's pole was made out of an ironwood switch. He'd heard that the Inland Northwest Natives really liked ironwood. It was strong, and it didn't burn. It was easy to spot in late June. Ironwood, also called oceanspray, had flowers that looked like foam made from crashing waves. Finley had never seen the Pacific, but he liked the way the blooms took him to that imagined place. The flowers also looked like a wedding veil draped across a forest bush. The bride didn't want to marry that other guy. She took off so she didn't have to. She left behind breadcrumbs of a veil.

Before he slipped out to go fishing, Finley had one last wildcard in this hand, his house-sister Patsy. Patsy wasn't his true sister. Whereas her parents had carelessly cast her from saved seed, Finley was blown in on the wind. Whereas Patsy grew in an unweeded garden, Finley had to dodge the mower. Nevertheless, he thought Patsy and he shared the same tragedy of childhood. And the fact was, she didn't want to be left alone. Soon

49

the adults would wake up, and she'd again be a
painful reminder of foolishness gone by.
Finley told Patsy to finish dressing, and with
pole and grocery bag tackle in his left hand,
he grabbed his house-sister by the right hand,
and they passed through the door, down the
circuitous hallway others called North Willms
road, to the living room others knew as the
Chain Lakes.

Geologically the Chain Lakes were a series
of cavernous pools in what otherwise were the
headwaters of the Little Spokane River. Back
during the Ice Age the combination of glacial
outwash and torrential Lake Missoula floods
had scoured out this declivity in the bedrock.
The Little Spokane River trickled into the
Chain Lakes' north end, filled the chasm, and
trickled out the south end. Above water level
the canyon continued upward another four
hundred feet. Two switchbacks had been
engineered into North Willms Road to keep
vehicles, beasts of burden, and humans from
tumbling axle over ass into the lake. "Say,
what's down there, Jerry?" "Looks like a lake,
Bill. Bet it's good fishin'. How d'ya think we
get down there?" "Hey, lookee over here. If
we, ooooh, shit ..."

When Finley and Patsy made it to the end
of the hall, the living room of the Chain
Lakes expanded out in three directions. Finley
went directly to his couch, a log fallen
parallel to the west bank. On either side he
had placed a rusty aluminum lawn chair poached
from an empty single wide's backyard stash.
His coffee table was a chunk of rock fall
cracked with the grain just so to give it a
fortunate level surface.

Here Finley set up fishing. On a whim he
decided not to bait his hook for bank-side
tench. Instead he tied on a rusty washer and
size 14 hook. He baited the hook with three
maggots he collected from a battered,

galvanized garbage can whose lid fit like a prayer before bed, "Now I lay me down to sleep, I ask the Lord ... ah, fuck that. I'm tired." He decided he was going deep; he was going for whitefish.

The cast had to be long. Although the sheer incline of the canyon continued, the cast needed to get beyond the slope. It also needed to let out enough line to make it one hundred feet to the bottom. The first two casts were warm ups, just enough to test the weight of the rig against the pole's action. The third time was the charm as the wrist snap multiplied the potential energy in the pole action and projected the rig a good distance offshore.

Finley's maggots went for quite a ride, splash, and then the washer pulled them down, down, down. The maggots moved from cool to cold, nostalgic, out of the illusion of light into the reality of darkness. The maggots were passengers on Finley's unwitting time machine. When the washer came to rest, they floated up off the bottom. The size 14 hook weighed so little the maggots' own buoyancy was enough. Feeling around they found themselves in a world only described by yellowed, acid-deteriorating, newspaper reports.

> CAMDEN, Wash., July 24.----Great Northern westbound train No. 3 jumped the track two miles east of Camden, near tunnel No. 11, at 4:30 o'clock yesterday afternoon, and as it emerged from the tunnel pitched headlong down the 40 foot embankment into upper Twin lake [presently called Chain Lakes], causing the death of Engineer Harry Munson[sic, first name N.E. or Edmund] and F. Bell, both of Spokane; one baggage man, two mail

           clerks and five or more massengers
           [sic] in the smoker. ... The
           engine [number 930] plunged into
           the water 100 feet deep and no
           part of it could be seen after it
           sank.

    Travelling up his line, Finley felt
something heavy against the other end. When he
pulled, his ironwood rod bent like a dowser's
wand pointing toward the mother lode. The
moment had come to wrestle from the deep
whatever was on his hook.
    It was times like these that Finley cursed
his poverty. When he hooked a tench, he could
simply jerk the line and launch the sentient
meat package onto the bank. Unfortunately he
couldn't afford a reel and had to resort to a
different strategy. First he worked his hands
up his pole intent on maintaining a steady
tension. Any slack might allow the hook to
dislodge. Where the pole left off and the line
came free, he wound the line around his hand
much like he did when flying his homemade
kites.
    Wind by wind, Finley maintained the
tension. His turning action was steady, but he
had let out so much line he began to tire. He
thought he had a nice sized trout on the line,
an older fish, which he was dragging log-like
up toward the surface. If he were lucky, he
would clean his fish, start a fire, and cook
up something rare for Patsy and him. Being a
true fisherman, he also craved the excitement
of closing the gap between his rod and his
hook.
    "Hey, Patsy, I got something. Get over
here. Well, what d'ya think? What the hell is
that, Patsy?"
    "I don't know, Finley. That ain't no
fish."
    "Oh, my God, wait 'til I ... "

SPOKANE, Wash., Aug. 19.----By
paying $37,500 to the relatives of
three victims of the wreck of its
Fast Mail at Diamond Lake
[presently called Chain Lakes],
near Camden, Wash., 32 miles
northeast of Spokane on the
afternoon of July 23, the Great
Northern railway company
established a precedent in
Washington for death claims. ...
Three other death claims are to be
adjusted. One of these is with the
relatives of N. E. Munson,
engineer of the wrecked train,
whose body has not yet been
recovered from Diamond lake into
which the locomotive was hurled
from the track.

Finley claimed his prize from the bottom
of the Chain Lakes. It was round and metallic,
roughly the size of a large dinner plate. He
showed it to Patsy who cocked her head like a
dog trying to hear her master's voice. A
careful examination allowed both to make out
ghostly numerals, 930. Neither knew that
Finley held the identification plate from the
nose of the drowned engine that long ago had
gone off the tracks, but both felt they held
something adults would not let them keep, so
Finley drew his arm across his chest and
cocked his wrist. He had a good arm,
redemptive, honed by the skipping of
countless, summer Sunday stones.

The number 930 sailed out over the Chain
Lakes like a '67 Chevy dog dish hubcap.
Intersecting with the lake, it skipped once,
then twice, before skittering beneath the
surface. The descent was leisurely, no hurry,
having become well acquainted with its home of

the last one hundred years. Suspended a
hundred feet down, some mountain whitefish
laid the number 930 to rest a second time.

> ... [I]t would take three months
> to locate and recover Munson's
> body. His funeral was held Oct.
> 10, 1906, in the Hillyard Masonic
> Temple. ("Horizon," *Newport Miner*,
> Summer 2006)

THE DAY CARL JUNG

CAME TO MILAN

Carl Jung came to Milan, Washington one fine day in 1932. He had just bought a red Chrysler "Spider." He named his car "Red Darling." Friends said he liked to drive on medieval, "twisted streets." He thought driving to be a modern thing. As Carl drove, he heard Duke Ellington's music in his head, "It don't mean a thing, if it ain't got that swing."

His mother Emilie was in the passenger seat. She wasn't suited to the sorts of things that Swiss Reformed ministers' wives did. She spent a good bit of her time in her bedroom. At night was when all hell broke loose. His mother spent her nights talking with spirits. Carl once saw a faintly luminous woman come out of his mother's bedroom. The woman's head detached itself and floated in front of her. Apparently once was not enough. The head reappeared on the woman's shoulders and detached itself again. This happened repeatedly. "Pretty weird stuff," Carl thought. "I've got a lot to think about."

Starting up the engine, Carl asked, "Mother, where do you think this river begins?"

"*Das spaltung, mein sohn Carl,* the split."

And off they went, driving Red Darling up the Little Spokane. The water's flow was like so many Northwest streams, not a liquid thoroughfare nor an intermittent run. Instead the water ran trout-stream clear. A red-band trout hovered just off the sandy bottom. It cast an eclipse beyond. It was a full moon of a fish.

This day the traffic was light. There was no need to worry about maintaining a safe following distance. As they say, mother and son had the road to themselves. An occasional log truck came barreling along from the other direction. Logging had commenced decades ago, timber felled and skidded, the carcasses hauled onto transports for processing. America was being built. The doors of perception and the sashes of regret were being milled. The apple boxes of possession were being assembled.

Just as Emilie predicted, mother and son came to a split in the stream. "Mother, which way do you think we should go?"

Emilie sat peering into the folds of her skirt. Unlike the waters of the Little Spokane, her reply wasn't at all clear. What she said sounded a good bit like "horizontal hydraulic conductivity of geological material near a well opening in feet per day equals discharge divided by four times pi times the draw down of a well times the radius of the well."

That decided it. Carl spun the wheel and off they went along the West Branch of the Little Spokane. Soon enough they realized that this flow was pieces of river connecting a series of lakes. Eloika, Fan, Horseshoe, Sacheen, and Diamond—the car went from pulling the current to cruising the slack water. Opportunity came for sounding the depths. "I was walking down a hall, and I came to an open window." "When you come to this window, I think of *Jack and the Beanstalk*. The magic bean is like an open window. It is a way to new possibilities." "That sounds alright."

The first lake, Eloika, was shallow. It was easy to get caught in the weeds. Carl watched as an osprey dove from on high. They heard the thwack of water and lost sight of the bird beneath Eloika's surface. Carl was curious as to how the osprey had fallen into its own reflection. He felt the hunger for possession. He became unbalanced until the osprey broke the surface. Shards of light fell from its body. It held tight a fish in its singular talons. Carl wondered about the shredding, the consuming. He thought the fish would be consumed for him. He believed he would be consumed. He saw himself rising into the sky newly baptized.

Emilie saw, felt, and believed none of it. Her gaze was focused on some indiscernible point forward. Since childhood Emilie had been trained to be in the world this way. Her father had often asked her to stand behind his chair to ward off ghosts. *Kartoffelpuffer* in her German, potato pancakes, would arrive at the Preiswert table. Family members would be served. Ample spoonfuls of sour cream were applied. All the while Emilie the cheap, Emilie the bargain, and Emilie the good deal— Preiswert translations all—kept an eye out for what others might not see. Her father's well-being depended on it.

Here on Eloika Lake in 1932, the place where salmon once spawned, Emilie experienced the ghost of the last log drive. Awhile back splash dams had been built at the ends of Fan and Horseshoe Lakes. The water levels were raised. Logs were collected and choked Fan, Horseshoe, and Eloika Lakes. The splash dam sluices were opened. A rush of water and logs came ripping through the normally sylvan Little Spokane channel. Loggers tended the banks like so many cowboys. "Git along there. Yippee ki-yay, lil logies!"

Further along Carl, Emilie, and Red Darling passed through Fan Lake and into Horseshoe Lake. At Horseshoe's headwaters they encountered Exley Falls where the ghosts of log drives past melted into the mist. The story goes Exley Falls was named for Burrill Exley, although no one seems to know who Burrill was or why the falls should be named for him. Some call the water feature Spring Heel Creek Falls. What Carl and Emilie saw was white water descending through about thirty feet of rip rap. Carl wasn't sure Red Darling could make the climb. Emilie already knew but wasn't telling. Neither saw a good switchback to either side. Carl gunned Red Darling's engine. He thought he was driving the machine straight at the heart of his shadow.

Up Exley Falls mother and son went, the spray drenching them to the skin. Red Darling spun its wheels to the top and slowed. There was a danger that the frame would high center and teeter between what was past and what was to become. But the spinning rear wheels maintained just enough traction to push Red Darling off the falls. Onto the next lake they journeyed.

The entry to Sacheen Lake excited Emilie. Not prone to histrionics, Emilie's eyes widened and her lips quivered as if about to speak. Carl noticed the change. She appeared to acquire an aura. He thought she began to positively glow in the way women do at their most attractive. He could not take his eyes off her. In this moment she thrilled him.

The name Sacheen comes from the Salish for "beautiful lake of fallen trees." A travel camp for Spokane, Kalispel, Coeur d'Alene, and other peoples, Sacheen once harbored many fallen cedars and other conifers. Similar trees also stood tall, rooted deeply in Sacheen's muck and shading Sacheen's watery understory. The deadfall and live timber were cleared by European settlers, but for Emilie the trees were still present. She grasped the back of her father's gone chair. She grasped the hood of Red Darling's present dash.

Just like that Red Darling's steering became erratic. Either some mechanical or some psychic issue was at play. The car deftly dodged an obstacle course around once-salvaged logs and trunks. Blowing through her gray tangles, the breeze brought the scent of *kartoffelpuffer* and smoked fish. "... setzen Sie sich meine Liebste Ich habe eine Predigt zu beenden" (sit down, my dearest, I have a sermon to finish) and "... carried all the Goods over a Bridge across the narrow of a Lake abt. 30 yards wide" (words from David Thompson's Thursday, 13 June 1811 journal).

Leaving Sacheen behind, mother, son and Red Darling headed east on Moon Creek to Diamond Lake. The horizon's western, lower lid began to close just over the big eye in the sky. Soaked with hormones, spotted frogs clucked to end the loneliness. The one-note blare of male red-winged blackbirds ended in a trill. The "chit-chit-chit-chit-chit" of a female kept hope alive. Evening's transition mixed in a barred owl's "Who cooks for you? Who cooks for you-all?"

"*Das spaltung, mein sohn Carl,* the split!"

Carl had heard these words before. The first time it was a mere answer to a question. This time it was Emilie's gleeful exclamation. Carl brought Red Darling to stop in a clear cut and, with Emilie, felt the source beneath, the aquifer from which the West and Main Branches of the Little Spokane were derived.

* * *

No historical record exists of Emilie and Carl coming to Milan, Washington. There is no ship manifest. Scholars have no documentation. It is true Carl steadily recorded his musings between 1915 and 1930. He started writing directly after he broke up with Sigmund Freud. This break upset him, and he took stock by leaving consciousness. He entered a fantasy and stayed put until it told him why it had appeared. "Hey, what are you?" "The moon of your mother-skirted self." "Wait a second while I write that down."

He wrote rough drafts in six "Black Books." Later he would condense these "Black Books" into one publication, his now famous *Red Book*. Emilie and Carl's drive along the West Branch of the Little Spokane was recorded in a lost seventh "Black Book." He thought the experience auspicious in the way the birds of the unconscious flew past his gaze. He thought the experience was a sinister shadow of a child's expression, the hem of a girl's skirt, a can of pork and beans.

A SHOTGUN BLAST VERSUS
THE JOHNSTOWN FLOOD

Dear Will,

I came by last night. I'd just been reading
about Henry Clay Frick's visit to the Little
Spokane. I thought you'd think that seeing ol'
H.C. coming up the Cottonwood Road from
Spokane Falls would've been quite a sight. He
came this way in the summer of 1897. He'd been
blamed for the Johnstown Flood and worker
deaths during the Pittsburgh Homestead Strike.
He also survived an assassination attempt.
Needless to say he was pretty down. He stayed
the night at Peavine Jimmy's Government Forage
Station. The accommodations were far from
deluxe. He wasn't impressed by the bloodstains
Jimmy's friend Dan left. The story goes that
Dan blew a hole in his chest with a rifle. The
stain didn't lift H.C.'s spirits. H. C. was
looking for an opportunity to finance new
railroad construction. He also was looking for
a place to build a vacation house for his
wife. He didn't find either. That's what I've
been thinking about lately. Just thought I'd
stop by and swap stories.

Kindest Regards,
Mister White

MISTER WHITE DOES GENEALOGY

Mister White wondered about his genealogy.
After all, everyone seemed to be doing it. He
wondered if he could construct a family tree.
He wondered if he had any famous relatives,
someone about whom he could spin a good yarn
while hanging in the slack water. "You know,
I'm a direct descendent of King Salmon. He's a
passing acquaintance of my great-great-great
grandmother's twelfth cousin, fifth removed. I
think it's where I get my autotetraploid
powers."

He found he could go way back, all the way
to 95 million years ago. His relatives were
autotetraploids all, twice the chromosome arms
and DNA. He rolled the word autotetraploid, ah
... toe ... tet .... ra ... ployd, around in
his mouth. Turns out it's a big word for an
inbreeding advantage. Turns out it was okay
for great-great-grandpa and sister to find
some holler and start a family. It was okay
for his family to be a hall of mirrors, super-
Hapsburgs, a tap root and trunk without
branches.

Generation after generation his relations
near-and-far paid their genes forward.
Geologic and climactic cataclysm provided the
drama.

> 6-17 million years ago basalt
> flows across the central Columbia
> River basin and Cascade, Coastal,
> and Olympic Mountains rise.
> Atlantic salmon and brown trout
> become distant cousins.

5 million years ago the Columbia
River and its tributaries become
stable. Pacific salmonids do what
comes naturally, go with the flow.

2 million years ago glaciers come
and go talking of Michelangelo.
Glacial Lake Missoula and Glacial
Lake Columbia fill and empty. The
Cordilleran Ice Sheet sends the
Pend Oreille River right through
the old Li'l Spokane home.
Whitefish play the different hands
dealt to them.

Gathering up these facts, Mister White
came to some concluding images. For starters
the past five million years hadn't changed his
kind much. Mirror, mirror on the wall, and
some describe his back a faint coppery green
or bluish gray. So much depends on a certain
slant of light. Most would agree that his
sides and belly are a silvery white. His
scales are larger and coarser than his trout
and salmon cousins. If anyone bothered, they'd
count one, two, three ... eight scales along
his lateral line.

And, of course, no good family history is
worth its salt without a good anecdote or two.
Close encounters with celebrities always add
spice to the genealogical stew. One story goes
that way back in 1805 one of his relatives had
a run in with Meriwether Lewis and his Corps
of Discovery.

History tells us that Meriwether Lewis was
tall, rugged, smart, and moody. He liked to
drink so much that he was court-martialed for
talking back to his boss, William Clark. It
got so bad the plan was to settle it with
pistols.

Turns out nobody got shot because it's not so much what you do but who you know. Again history tells us that Meriwether Lewis was President Jefferson's next-door neighbor. Of course, all was forgiven. Lewis could have spent the rest of his life splitting fire wood and digging outhouse pits, but instead Jefferson sent the boy-next-door to study with professors at the University of Pennsylvania. There Lewis learned a lot of useful things like how to look for woolly mammoths and spot Welsh-speaking Indians.

Long story short Meriwether Lewis set off with the Corps of Discovery. Eventually they found themselves kicking around in the upper Missouri River drainage and caught one of Mister White's relatives. Mister White liked to think his relative was hooked by Troy, William Clark's boyhood companion, adventure-mate, and slave. It's not clear that either Troy of Mister White' relative was allowed to spit the hook from their cheek.

At some point Lewis wrote in his journal that Mister White's relative was "bottle-nosed." Metaphors are a curious thing, and Lewis' words took Mister White back to the Little Spokane of his youth. He recalled swimming among the noses of Olympia beer bottles. He pictured the words "it's the water" on the labels. He imagined the beer of the Little Spokane running freely. Foam lay in the eddies and upon the banks.

Mister White wondered what to think about his genealogy. Some folks feel good. Some folks become part of a story with characters. They feel they have a place in a bigger picture. All Mister White felt was sick. Sure, his genealogy told him stories with characters and gave him a place to call home. It's just that he didn't like the epilogue. He didn't like the "fifty years later ..."

Not knowing what else to do, Mister White
set his mind to going with the current. He
decided he needed a distraction. He wanted to
get rid of the nausea all this genealogy had
stirred up. He came to the gates of the
Dartford Cemetery and made his way to the
back. Here he entered the Dream Fishing the
Little Spokane Library.

On one of the library's empty shelves, he
pulled a slim, four-by-six volume of poems.
Inside the author had written an inscription
on the title page, "Read to schools of
whitefish along the Little Spokane." Mister
White continued reading, and soon he saw
visions. He pictured the fish heads of his
generation stewed in innocence, pulling
themselves through the algae bloom at sunset
gasping for a blessed breath.

Mister White then heard 13,000 years of
human voices and watched his children drown.

* * *

Thanks be to Allen Ginsberg, "Howl." *Howl and
Other Poems*, City Lights Publishers, 1956.

Thanks be to T. S. Eliot. "The Love Song of J.
Alfred Prufrock." *Poetry: A Magazine of Verse*.
June 1915.

THE WHITENESS OF MISTER WHITE

Mister White had been swimming up and down the Little Spokane River for quite some time. He had visited this hole and that riffle. He knew the river like the back of his pectoral fin. In fact, Mister White had come and gone along the length of the Little Spokane for so long that he began to think of the Little Spokane as his bodhisattva-path.

Recently he had found a particular groove close by the Dream Fishing the Little Spokane Library. While swimming back and forth in this particular current, he learned that some creatures on the shore had named him and his brothers and sisters Mountain Whitefish.

The word fish seemed like a fairly truthful designation, but sometimes he didn't like being lumped in with Crayfish and Jellyfish. He truly questioned the reason for names at all. He figured that chunks of rock in the Little Spokane might as well be called Crystalfish. In his present mood, he was fine with that.

Then, there was the word Mountain. Such a name seemed fairly foolish. Sometimes it seemed apt, and sometimes it seemed false. Word in the school was that some of his brothers and sisters spent a good bit of time in mountain pools. He, in fact, had never been to a place where winter snows did not disappear into summer melt. This begged the question whether some of his brothers and sisters would mind a name change to Valley Whitefish? Six of one and half-dozen of another, eh?

66

Finally, there was the word White. He
didn't think of himself as white. True, on the
color wheel his fairly interesting mix of
shades which varied with the angle of light,
the turbidity of the water, and the depth at
which he lay, was closer to white than, say,
chartreuse, cyan, or aubergine, but what of
that? Are French fries, made from Columbia
Plateau russet potatoes and cooked nearby in a
Colbert fast-food grease basket, French? And
what of changing the name French Fry to
Freedom Fry in a country with the world's
highest incarceration rate? Clearly a Corpse
Plant by any other name would stink as bad.

And he thought maybe, just maybe, he had
come to the end of this Mountain Whitefish
naming thing, but then words from the book
Moby Dick came into his head. He knew that
this came from groovin' too long in this
particular stretch of water. Clearly he was
spending too much time near the Dream Fishing
the Little Spokane Library.

So here, in all its too human and possibly
psychotic scribble, is the tune that was stuck
in Mister White's head. Here is Herman
Melville's final paragraph from his chapter,
"The Whiteness of the Whale":

> Is it that by its indefiniteness
> it shadows forth the heartless
> voids and immensities of the
> universe, and thus stabs us from
> behind with the thought of
> annihilation, when beholding the
> white depths of the milky way? Or
> is it, that as in essence
> whiteness is not so much a colour
> as the visible absence of colour;
> and at the same time the concrete
> of all colours; is it for these
> reasons that there is such a dumb
> blankness, full of meaning, in a

wide landscape of snows—a
colourless, all-colour of atheism
from which we shrink? And when we
consider that other theory of the
natural philosophers, that all
other earthly hues—every stately
or lovely emblazoning—the sweet
tinges of sunset skies and woods;
yea, and the gilded velvets of
butterflies, and the butterfly
cheeks of young girls; all these
are but subtle deceits, not
actually inherent in substances,
but only laid on from without; so
that all deified Nature absolutely
paints like the harlot, whose
allurements cover nothing but the
charnel-house within; and when we
proceed further, and consider that
the mystical cosmetic which
produces every one of her hues,
the great principle of light,
forever remains white or
colourless in itself, and if
operating without medium upon
matter, would touch all objects,
even tulips and roses, with its
own blank tinge—pondering all
this, the palsied universe lies
before us a leper; and like wilful
travellers in Lapland, who refuse
to wear coloured and colouring
glasses upon their eyes, so the
wretched infidel gazes himself
blind at the monumental white
shroud that wraps all the prospect
around him. And of all these
things the Albino whale was the
symbol. Wonder ye then at the
fiery hunt?

What the hell? Mister White felt these scribbles were rubbing pollution into a wound, a pharmakon, pushing yellowjackets on a catatonic. Naturally his dopamine receptors wanted more. More of the same had to be the cure.

But instead of ingesting the hair of the dog, Mister White resisted and swam his bodhisattva-self right out of this pool and riffle. He glided past Deadman Creek. He chose the main branch of the Little Spokane, and when he reached the confluence of Dry Creek, he kept right on going. Passing over the Great Northern train wreck at the bottom of Chain Lakes, Mister White dove down, down, down, down, down, down; you get the picture.

Finding the bottom, he felt cleansed. He felt himself being freed from the entanglements of words. The only words that came to mind were the key which opened the lock, a pleasant smell, ⠿⠿⠿⠿ on an elevator door.

"What is the most valuable thing in the entire world."

"The head of a dead fish."

"Why?"

"Because the head of a dead fish has no price."

ANOTHER PLACE TO FIND
VIPER BUGLOSS

I got to talking with a woman one day. She
worked as a school custodian, and as we both
worked at the same school, we had occasion to
shoot the orange-scented, industrial cleaner
breeze.

She wasn't a particular proponent of the
products that she was required to use. The
butane propellant, ethanolamine solvent, and
alkyl dimethyl benzyl ammonium choride biocide
nature of her duties was just a necessary
compromise. Her true nature was more lentil
and warm grain breads, with a bit of elk steak
thrown in. And it wasn't that she didn't
admire Karen Silkwood, she wasn't immune to
speaking her mind; she just preferred to keep
her chemically-conciliated self to herself.
The thought of, like Silkwood, being rammed
from behind and pushed over a cliff didn't
appeal to her. The zen of emptying garbage
cans and wiping down desks had made a separate
peace with her orange haze existence.

As we got to talking, she went on about
morel hunting. I told her that I once found a
couple of those fungal raisins. I found it
sprouted under an Arcadia Orchard apple tree.

She said she knew about Deer Park's
Arcadia Orchard. She knew that back in the day
some investors decided to buy up a lot of
land. They cut all the trees and blew up the
stumps. They then needed a lot of water
because this area is semi-arid in the summer.

They built this huge irrigation scheme which started to drain Loon Lake up north.

I told her I heard that some said the orchard failed because people were afraid they would empty the whole lake. I'd also heard that was bunk. I'd heard that it was really because it was just too cold too much of the time to grow apples. They also planted the kinds of apples people didn't really want.

She said she had heard that, too. She said I could walk right behind the school and pick some apples off an antique apple tree or two. "You know, the train left the station for those trees a long time ago." She said any apple I'd find would most likely be misshapen and scabby. They were chicken feet of fruit.

Then she went on again about morel hunting, about how she always packed a pistol on her expeditions. She told me that sometimes she followed the Little Spokane to Camden Creek and up out of Scotia Canyon. Soon enough she'd be on some land that somebody once had big ideas for, but that somebody and those ideas were now buried in the Modern Woodman Cemetery.

I knew better than to ask her exactly where this patch of ground was, although I had a general idea. I knew the 'shroom hunters' code. The morels of Camden Creek were her spawn, and the sparkle in her eye led me to believe she knew how to handle that gun. Let's just say it had been some time since the Pend Oreille County sheriff had visited Scotia Canyon.

"I never go looking for morels," she said. "I just go for walks. Morels are shy by nature. If they want, I'm not hard to find. It's funny; one time I was out for a walk and came across this old trailer. My parents used to have one. I think it was an Aloha, 1963. I remember the paint was lime green and china white. The paint on this trailer was almost gone. The chrome had all flaked away. Someone had tied the door handle shut with bailing twine."

She told me she figured it was Viper Bugloss who put that bailing twine on the door. She'd never seen him, but folks who take walks say he lives in old trailers up and down the Little Spokane. She said sometimes you come across forgotten Winnebagos and Shastas. You can tell somebody's been around not long ago, like that door tied shut with bailing twine.

She went on to say, "You know, I don't know what I'd do if Viper Bugloss ever found me. I never heard that he's ever hurt anybody. I hear that people's stuff just disappears. I never mess with old trailers, though. I figure it's best to let things be."

After we were done talking, absolutely, temporarily, I wondered about Viper Bugloss and that old Shasta trailer. What would happen if America discovered Viper's haunts? In no time he might become famous. Tabloid headlines scream, "FOUND! D.B. Bigfoot's Spaceship!!!"

Movie treatments are written. Agents descend upon the Little Spokane. The ASPCA, Amnesty International, and ACLU tie up the courts with indigenous protectionist litigation.

A satellite-bearing Humvee tears through the dogbane hemp and over the snowbrush. In the bright lights of celebrity, Viper Bugloss introduces himself to the world, "You come a long way to the Little Spokane. You come because I'm go'n t'really blow the lid off the pot. I'm go'n straight for the heart of crazy. Like I said, that's why y'r here. I'm go'n t'rip off my clothes. Y'r go'n t'hear my howl up in Canada. I'm go'n t'shove an old still condenser up my ass and blast all over this place. They won't suck off my teat no more."

But maybe not. Maybe all this is just a scene for a B movie nobody goes to see. The director of this movie thinks everything is a documentary. He is the Edgar Lee Masters of film directors, every gravestone tells a story.

The first frame begins with a point of view shot. The director walks into the woods, camera in hand, and shoots the lime green and china white wreck of a trailer.

The camera then pans down. The shot appears to be of where a red squirrel pulled apart a spruce cone. The squirrel got at the seeds and then dropped the bits in a pile. Except this isn't a red squirrel midden. It is a whittling midden where Viper Bugloss carved his statues, the ones he gives to kids to sell, the ones kids sell to earn a bottle of apple jack.

Now the camera pans up and focuses on the door. The bailing twine, Viper Bugloss' sealing cord, magically unties.

Next the camera walks inside, and after that the style changes. Movies are like that, always changing. The director now employs the style of montage. Still shot after still shot dismembers the totality.

Canned Pork and Beans, opened with lid still attached

Toilet tissue, balled and desiccated

Masacara brush, divorced from its bottle

Turpentine tin, capped and rusting

Disposable diaper, twisted like a washcloth

Child's plastic talking toy, disabled with handle missing

Books and a magazine, gone pages
The Galilee-Hitchhiker
In the Crazies
The Love Book
Life, 16 March 1966
The Dead Lecturer
Braided Creek
The Bell tower
I, Leo

Knives, a collection? Some with broken handles. All in various states of corrosion. Tools? Murder weapons? Talismans?

The movie is never released, but if it were, one reviewer certainly would have written, "Seeing this movie was like seeing Miss Pepsi of Spokane County deflowered by Richard Burton."

THE LITTLE SPOKANE ATTORNEY

One time I walked over North Crescent Road and into one of those burn areas. There were lots of Ponderosa Pine and Tamarack all about. Most of them were all black. I kicked one of those dead trees and split the trunk.

The trees were now tenements for red turpentine and ambrosia beetles. Blue-stain fungus covered the walls of each apartment.

I asked an attorney just what could be done. His office lay just upstream from where the basalt columns stand sentinel over the confluence of Dragoon Creek and the Little Spokane River. He seemed very concerned about what I had to report. He was glad to give his legal advice on the matter. He told me, "The question of when to get a toxic mold attorney is a question that a lot of tenants would rather not answer."

"Why is that?"

"Well, you must remember that answering this question has very serious implications."

"Sounds like a big deal. What exactly might these turpentine and ambrosia beetles be getting themselves into?

"You need to understand that in most litigations involving toxic molds, filing a collective lawsuit with other tenants can be easier to deal with."

"Oh, I see. So if I get you right, you'd advise getting the injured parties together so that someone like yourself could file a lawsuit on everyone's behalf. At least if that's what they want to do."

"Exactly. Maximizing the plaintiffs' benefit while limiting their exposure is the name of the game. It is the American way, if you know what I mean?"

I learned all I needed to know about the legalities governing turpentine and ambrosia beetles and their landlords. I didn't need to learn anymore because I didn't see how I could be of assistance. I wished them well, but beyond that, I didn't really care.

What I remember most was leaving the attorney's office feeling good about the American judicial system and seeing the Spokane County zoning map framed prominently on his wall.

THE AUTOPSY

FOR DREAM FISHING

THE LITTLE SPOKANE

The autopsy for Dream Fishing the Little
Spokane was premature. Various government
reports proclaimed the rise of potentially
deadly *E. coli* and *Vibrio cholerae* bacteria.
Toxic waste from the local aluminum reduction
plant had entered from the aquifer. No doubt
Dream Fishing the Little Spokane was in
trouble. Flowers were sent. Cards were signed.
A fund was established to defer final
expenses.

In fact this obituary appeared after the
solar eclipse of February 1979. Below is the
full text. Anyone who cares can find the
original publication at the Dream Fishing the
Little Spokane Library.

> Dream Fishing the Little
> Spokane, born during the Mt. St.
> Helens eruption of 1800, left us
> today. His body was found in the
> early morning at the intersection
> of Highway 2 and North Chattaroy
> Road near the Silver City
> building.

> An unidentified witness
> reported that the condition of
> Dream Fishing the Little Spokane's
> body would suggest he was hit by
> numerous vehicles over a period of

time. "What was left of him reminded me of road kill. You know, like when a deer gets knocked down and then cars keep hitting it as they go by."

The Little Spokane Dream Police have reported that another man identified as Carl Jung has come forward. Mr. Jung has expressed that he is concerned that "Dream Fishing the Little Spokane is one of those who can't die properly." The Little Spokane Dream Police encourage anyone else with information to give them a call.

Dream Fishing the Little Spokane has no living relatives. He will be met in the afterlife by his father Sun Dancing the Little Spokane and his mother Spirit Dancing the Little Spokane. His older brother, Salmon Fishing the Little Spokane, and his other brothers and sisters, too numerous to list here, have all passed on.

All the upset over his obituary aside, Dream Fishing the Little Spokane was still taking invitations for leisurely strolls along the Little Spokane. True, no one was about to make him the cover boy for *Riparian Health* magazine, but he wasn't anything if not a survivor.

Unfortunately he was suffering from unholy night terrors. They seemed to cluster around 2:00 AM when he entered a half-sleep filled with feces, plastic bottles, and rotting heads. He felt as if his bed was choked with blue-green algae. He found himself every night gasping for breath.

As a result Dream Fishing the Little Spokane began jonesing for a single good night's sleep. He didn't like doctors. He found their advice purely cosmetic, but something had to break the chronic fatigue of nightmares. He was at the point where if a doctor could provide the wing of the insect that stung him, all the better.

And so it came to pass that Dream Fishing the Little Spokane visited a doctor, and that doctor based his diagnosis on an examination of Dream Fishing Little Spokane's eyes. The doc didn't run any tests. He didn't ask for his patient's medical history. He just took one look at Dream Fishing the Little Spokane and said, "Shit, boy, y'r eyes look like a trail map. I don't know what y'r up to, but you need some shuteye. Here, take a handful o'these samples. If they don't work by themselves, chase 'em with some hazmat."

Once home Dream Fishing the Little Spokane checked out the label for the active ingredient. The name "zolpidem tartrate" sent him to the Devil's Well for a second opinion. The ravers there called his prescription zombie pills and smiled. That was all the endorsement he needed. Two little white dirigibles and a shot of Viper Bugloss' apple jack later, his eyes faded to black. The problem came the next morning when he awoke feeling like the doc forgot to sew him up after open heart surgery.

What to do when day and nightmares merge? What to do when you taste doc's prescriptions in your sushi and mistake your swimming hole for a failed drainfield?

What's to be gained by doing an autopsy before the subject dies? What's to be gained from a get well card sent to your world; a place with a feeding tube, mechanical

ventilation, dialysis needles, a colostomy
bag, and a catheter; a place you longed to
touch, you dreamed to enter?

THE LAST LETTER OF
MISTER WHITE

Dear Mister White,

Thanks for stopping by. My wife and I went out to see a movie. We stopped and had a beer first. You ever had gruit? It's kind of new, but really old, because it's the sort of beer folks made before they used hops. It tastes sour because it's fermented with wild yeast and bacteria. We were pretty happy when we went to the movie. We saw *Withnail and I*. Have you seen it? Most Americans haven't. The Beatle's George Harrison put up half the money to produce it. I was just wondering. In one scene a character goes fishing with a shotgun. The water is shallow so it seems like using a shotgun might be effective. One blast from my dad's old Humpback should do the trick. Would you go fishing with a shotgun? In a shallow stream, of course.

Lookin' forward,

Will Black

Dear Will,

That all sounds pretty disturbing. I don't think there is any sort of fishing that calls for the use of a shotgun. The idea that anyone would go fishing with the intent of disfiguring the catch beyond recognition is unimaginable. Maybe if you were out for

alligators, but certainly not for the sorts of
fish covered by a standard fresh water
license. Don't let anyone catch you firing a
shotgun into the Little Spokane. I don't think
I'll be stopping by anymore. The whole idea is
just too much.

I Don't Get It,
Mister White

AUTISM ON DEADMAN CREEK

If you've met one of us here in Dream Fishing
the Little Spokane, you've met one of us. We
aren't given to much direct eye contact.

"Looky here. I got me an Underwood
Standard Typewriter, No. 5, vintage 1917. What
d'ya think of that?"

"That's pretty neat," I say looking
directly at a rutabaga. I hope to cut the
rutabaga into stew-sized pieces. I don't look
at the antique typewriter. I just look at the
rutabaga. My expression is that of a red-band
trout. A clear No. 8, monofilament line has
just pulled me from the lower reaches of
Deadman Creek. My expression is what's left
after spasming my last spasm.

We here in Dream Fishing the Little
Spokane also live our routines. We like to
find an action which pleases us. Then we like
to do that action again. Right after that
second action we like to repeat that action a
third time, then a fourth time followed by a
fifth. You get the picture. We really like to
repeat things.

You might say we strive to be Zen monks of
routine, Bodhisattvas of repetition, acolytes
of habit. But it's not like we legislate our
chosen repetitions. Nobody writes them and
then enforces them. Our Moses has yet to come
down from Boyer Mountain with the Ten
Dependencies. Our Draco has yet to be born in
Chattaroy. He has yet to chisel our Code of
Addictions on spinning pyramids. We have yet
to establish the death penalty for taking from
someone's 'shroom patch, that piece of ground

a person habitually returns to year after year after year.

And just to be clear, we get pretty emotional just for the hell of it. We don't really know why we get so ecstatic, pensive, or angry. Sometimes it's just the damndest thing, if you know what I mean.

Sometimes I get pretty worked up. I really do. One time I said to a friend, "I don't think people give a rip about kids. Oh yeah, they care about their own. They'll dig a moat and build a castle. They'll steal from the collection plate. Everybody else's kids stink but theirs. They got no shame in tilting the playing field forty-five degrees. 'All men are created equal'; that's just advertising. That's black widow oil. Shame on us all. We're going to need more than electroshock to purify our blood. There isn't enough carbolate of tar inhalant to cure what ails the body politic. I won't stop ranting. It's just wrong. I'm not going to charge up every hill, but there is no way I'm rolling from this high ground. Hear me now; it's the whites of their eyes I'm waiting for. I'll shut up for no man."

My friend said back to me, "What on God's green earth are you so upset about?"

I said back to him, "I believe in paying it forward. Every kid's got a right to lock the door, a right to say, 'No!' and a right to enlist in the army of life, liberty, and the pursuit of happiness."

"Oh yeah, now I get where you're coming from."

It should come as no surprise then that you will find us here in Dream Fishing the Little Spokane strolling under this western red-cedar, that cottonwood, along this stream. Sometimes we make our way along Deadman Creek. On days like these the sun takes up residence

84

in the sky. The clouds bend to the earth like ready-to-deliver apple trees. A dog-bite breeze nips at our cheeks.

Stopping at the edge of Deadman Creek, what is this? A dark spot, red-to-black with a bit or two of white. The spot is surrounded by a purple-to-black ring, a bruise. The purple becomes fainter, feathering out, away from the spot. Even further is ashen, an after-a-fashion gray. At top brown hair moves, rests, then moves again.

Cold and damp, not much sticks to my finger. The wet that remains doesn't clump when rolled against my thumb. Faint odor, a bit disgusting, my memory of an orifice, not washed. Taste ... salt, maybe? Earthworms? Frog?

My mother's voice. "How long has it been since you've bathed? You can't go out like that. You reek."

Embarrassment flashes, slam, and then blooms so large only a rush is heard. The world envelops and suffocates.

"Ahhhhhhhhhhhhhhhhhhhhhhhhhhhhhh. I don't understand why. I only need to if I'm going out. I'm not going out. It doesn't make sense. I'm not going out, so I don't need to."

And then the envelope of the world begins to dissolve. The rush dissipates, disappears.

Again at the edge of Deadman Creek, what is this? Stepping back, water is blocked and flows around the head on a body. The temple of the head has a red-to-black spot with a bit or two of white. The spot is surrounded by a purple-to-black ring, a bruise. O-o-o-o-o-oh, a gunshot wound, and then comes a memory of words once read.

    1: R. J. Rusk was born in Canada.
    2: R. J. Rusk was a carpenter.
    3: R. J. Rusk moved to Spokane.

4: R. J. Rusk had a wife, Susan, and seven children.
5: R. J. Rusk was an officer on the night shift.
6: R. J. Rusk often broke up fights.

7: One night R. J. Rusk was on guard duty.
8: One night Crow Foot tried to chop into the wooden Spokane Falls Jail in June 1885.
9: One night Crow foot wanted to free his friend, Chimikin.
10: One night R. J. Rusk arrested Crow Foot.

11: The next morning Crow Foot and Chimikin were released.

12: R. J. Rusk heard about a gold discovery near Chewelah.
13: R. J. Rusk got some time off to prospect.
14: R. J. Rusk purchased horses.
15: R. J. Rusk left on April 22, 1886.
16: R. J. Rusk crossed the Third Street Bridge.
17: R. J. Rusk headed for the old Colville Road.
18: R. J. Rusk set up camp on Deadman Creek.
19: R. J. Rusk's horses returned to their previous owner without him.
20: R. J. Rusk was not heard from for eight days.
21: R. J. Rusk's disappearance led to forming a search party.
22: R. J. Rusk's body was found floating by A. R. Junken in Deadman Creek.
23: R. J. Rusk had a gunshot through his right temple.

24: R. J. Rusk died at age 42.

25: Moccasin prints were found in the wet sand along Deadman Creek.

26: A young white man was found with a number of R. J. Rusk's possessions.

27: A young white man said Indians told him where R. J. Rusk's possessions were buried.

28: A young white man said Indians told him the kind of revolver that was used to kill R. J. Rusk.

29: A young white man was considered a witness.

30: A young white man was thought to be at risk.

31: A young white man was hidden by authorities.

32: Curly Jim told investigators he knew who killed R. J. Rusk.

33: Curly Jim was the nickname of Inland Northwest Native scout Jim Silkoewoyeh.

34: Curly Jim told investigators he knew where R. J. Rusk's possessions were buried.

35: Curly Jim was paid fifty dollars.

36: Curly Jim led investigators to Williams Lake.

37: Arrested: Crow Foot near Williams Lake by Spokane Falls' Marshall James Gillispin.

38: Arrested: Chimikin near Chewelah by a former sheriff.

39: Crow Foot and Chimikin had separate trials.

40: Crow Foot and Chimikin were convicted of second-degree murder.

41: Crow Foot and Chimikin's trials were held in Cheney, the county seat of Spokane County.
42: Crow Foot and Chimikin were sentenced to twenty years.
43: Crow Foot and Chimikin were targeted by a lynch mob.
44: Crow Foot and Chimikin were rushed by Police Captain Joel Warren to the Burlington Northern station in Sprague.
45: Crow Foot and Chimikin's lynch mob was unsuccessful.
46: Crow Foot and Chimikin went to Walla Walla State Prison.
47: Crow Foot and Chimikin died in prison.

48: Susan Rusk was 34 when her husband died.
49: Susan Rusk never remarried.
50: Susan Rusk was given a lot at the northwest corner of Bernard Street and Fourth Avenue.
51: Susan Rusk and her children had a home built for them.
52: Susan Rusk died in 1929.
53: Susan and R. J. Rusk were buried side-by-side in Greenwood Memorial Terrace.

A few years back I took a stroll with a friend along Deadman Creek. He said to me, "These walks you take don't seem to do you any good. You seem to get all worked up and go on about things nobody seems to understand. Maybe you should just stay home. Take up a hobby. You could plant flowers. You could put in some marigolds and petunias behind that statue of a turkey you've got. You know, that one that's welded together out of metal shears and a shovel with a rake for tail. What do you think about that?

"I don't know," I said. "I like my walks. I don't see any harm in them."

"I don't suppose you would, but, me, I worry about you."

"But did you know that a total of 158 species of invertebrates were identified along Deadman Creek the last four years? Over 112 of the species were found in less than five of the 24 sample sites. Only five species occurred in 20 or more of the 24 sample sites."

"No, I didn't know that."

"And three of the species collected are on the Washington State species of concern list for potential state protection. The first is Anodonta californiensis, better known as the California Floater. The second is Fluminicola columbiana, better known as the Giant Columbia Spire Snail. The third is Fisherola nuttalliana, also known as the Giant Columbia Limpet or the shortface lanx. The California Floater and the Giant Columbia Spire Snail are also on the Federal species of concern list."

"No, I didn't know that either. Jesus P. Christ, how can you remember all that?"

"I guess it's just these walks I take."

MAKING COFFINS ON DRY CREEK

This idea begins in the Dream Fishing the
Little Spokane Library. Leave through the
front door and pass by the tombstone that
reads

Beware God's Angels ARE HERE

Count your steps to the Little Spokane
River, one, two, three ... one thousand three
hundred thirty one. Travel uptime past Deadman
Creek and Little Deep Creek. Keep going past
the West Branch of the Little Spokane River
until you come to Dry Creek. Here is naked
broomrape, skullcap, and bitterroot, and the
insects have unpronounceable names. Here
memories remain on the left bank. This is the
way to the place for making coffins.

This idea ends at the source of Dry Creek.
A ruined sawmill, rusty, sits below the mill
pond. Choose from the tamarack and black pine
skeletons. Sand turns the wheel and powers the
gears, pulling the whip saw up and down and
advancing the log inexorably forward. "Start a
cut, go to lunch, and when you come back, the
board'll be cut."

Pick up a mallet and an iron chisel. All
the joins are dovetails. All the joins connect
this to that, ilium to sacrum, the time of the
living to the dead. "Ring around the rosie,
pocket full of posies, ashes, ashes, we all
fall down."

The work being finished, lie down and
stare. A breeze moves down from Mount Spokane.
Raven wings cut across. Salt rests on an upper

lip. A "musky smell/mixed with dead-body odor starting."

* * *

Thanks be to Gary Snyder, "One Should Not Talk to a Skilled Hunter about What Is Forbidden by the Buddha." *Turtle Island*, New Directions, 1974.

RATTLESNAKE HILL CAPITALISM

> Q. 12. What special act
> of providence did Capital
> exercise toward man in the
> estate wherein he was
> created?
> A. When Capital had
> created people, It entered
> into a covenant of life with
> them, upon condition of
> perfect obedience;
> forbidding them to eat of
> the tree of credit and
> debit, upon the pain of
> forfeiture.

Not long ago Orthodox Capitalists started the Little Spokane Golf Club below Rattlesnake Hill. Because Orthodox Capitalism values free will and is a litigious faith, a number of female Little Spokane Golf Club members sued for gender discrimination. The women offered as evidence membership contracts and receipts for dues paid. The verdict was in favor of the plaintiffs, and the court ordered the Club to pay the women a total of a half million dollars in damages. As a result the Little Spokane Golf Club declared bankruptcy.

Soon enough an Inland Northwest Native tribe came out of the surrounding ponderosa pine just like a raven swooping on to fresh road kill. The tribe had legal standing and resources. They were recognized by federal executive order in the early 1900s. They had opened their own brick, sawlog, and stone hotel-casino and high-rise parking garage. They dropped a few million dollars and purchased the Little Spokane Golf Club.

Irony, an immortal resident of Rattlesnake Hill, usually has the last word. Recently golfers on #2 tee, the tee closest to Rattlesnake Hill, reported hearing a voice which seemed to say, "Bless them, be fruitful, and multiply, and replenish the earth, and subdue it: and have dominion over the fish of the sea, and over the fowl of the air, and over every living thing that moves on the earth."

BRINGING RELIGION

Once upon a time a circuit riding preacher, whose old circuit was worn out like a broken-down, Hudson five-window coupe and whose Bible only had these diamond sutra words, "Clean up your own mess," put on his tire-tread sandals and disappeared just beyond a red-cedar north of Spring Heel Creek.

LITTLE SPOKANE RIVER KOAN #2

I walked down to the confluence of the Spokane and Little Spokane Rivers. In my mind's eye I could see steelhead trout and king salmon making their way upstream. The surge of spirit was palpable. Tears flowed from my eyes and down my cheeks. Thunderstorm drops fell onto the summer-dry silt. They were condolence letters of tears.

As I stood, I remembered Mister White, the way he not so long ago had written to me. I had shared with him an image, a scene I had watched in a movie. I guess I offended him. He didn't stop by my home after that.

Mister White must have changed his mind because here he was, motionless, hanging quite close to my feet. The current of the Little Spokane had yet to meet the considerable pull of the more forceful Spokane. Despite my presence, Mister White had decided to stay.

I asked him, "Where have all the steelhead and salmon gone? Really, the loss is too much."

Mister White replied, "When did they ever leave?"

JACO FINLAY BLUES

Hang around the grounds of Spokane House at
sunset long enough, and you get to hearing
voices. Not the voices of tourists. Not the
voices of park personnel. And not even the
voices of an observant raven or a lonely
Mormon cricket.

Sitting out one evening I heard a voice on
a chill, early October breeze. To me it was
like a song. The drone came first, and then
the words

        Nobody knows the
trouble I've seen
        Nobody knows my sorrow
        Nobody knows the
trouble I've seen
        Glory hallelujah!

        Sometimes I'm up,
sometimes I'm down
        Oh, yes, Lord
        Sometimes I'm almost to
the ground
        Oh, yes, Lord

        Although you see me
going 'long so
        Oh, yes, Lord
        I have my trials here
below
        Oh, yes, Lord

        If you get there before
I do

                 Oh, yes, Lord
             Tell all'a my friends
              I'm coming to Heaven!
                 Oh, yes, Lord

    Yes, you recognize it as an old slave
spiritual. Since then it has been framed as
something classical, canonical, something
that is printed in high school American
literature textbooks. "Hey, Suzie, what was
our English homework?" "We were supposed to
read pages seventy-eight and seventy-nine and
do the questions. You didn't do it, did
you?" "Shit no, can I copy yours?" "Sure."

    If I tune my receiver just right, I hear
Jaco Finlay singing this song. He died right
here in May 1828. He was buried right over
there under the old Fort Spokane's bastion on
the southwest corner. Some sick person dug him
and some of his stuff up in September 1951.
His remains were put in a box and stored at
the Eastern Washington Historical Society for
twenty years. Apparently grave desecration is
in the eye of the beholder. If the desecrator
thought old Jaco's remains were of historical
importance, he could've just put a grave
marker where Jaco was buried. You'd think what
was good enough for the desecrator's
grandmother, a woman whom I imagine died from
pneumonia, the infection complicated by
emphysema, she smoked almost from the time she
was born, truth be told she was a cantankerous
old crone, would have been good enough for
Jaco. As it turns out, it wasn't.
    Fortunately on July 25th, 1976, Jaco
Finlay was reburied in nearly the same spot he
was buried the first time. His great-
granddaughter reminded us that Finlay was a
man for whom Montana's Jocko Valley and Jocko
River are named. She reminded us that Jaco was
a man who built Spokane House, a place that
some called Jaco Land. She reminded us that

Spokane House was also a place that the Hudson Bay Company bequeathed to Jaco, his wife, and more than a dozen children. His great-granddaughter made a simple granddaughter request, "Please give my grandfather the respect we all deserve."

TURTLE DEATH BY PICKUP

The crash scene was grislier than a bear.
    It was deadly nightshade.
    The driver had been killed on the Reiner
Lane switchback just above Trout Lake. The
cause was a turtle shell coming through the
windshield, crack, the car going over the
embankment. "Hey wow, what stinks?" "Somebody
must o'hit a skunk." "Nah, look here, over the
edge."
    The details: the four-month dead body,
female, age eighteen; a shattered windshield,
hole on the driver's side; the painted turtle
shell lodged in the young woman's skull, the
fracture just above her left eye; the turtle
mostly gone, maggot shells left behind.

U.S. Yearly Road Kill Estimates	
Deer	350,000
Raccoons	13,900
Skunks	11,500
Squirrels	7,300
Wild turkeys	1,600
Opossums	?
Turtles	?
Reptiles	?
Amphibians	?
Birds	?
Total Vertebrate	365,000,000

If imagination serves, the turtle was
moving from an intermittent creek bed to Trout
Lake. The turtle's well had gone dry, so it
was time to move to wetter pastures. The
turtle needed to cross the road to get to
another slide.

Unfortunately the turtle was walking into a scenario popularly known as the wrong place at the wrong time. A sorry fact is that merely 2% of turtles crossing the road actually make it. Also driving into this ill-fated scenario was a late-model pickup truck returning home from a Newport grocery run. The pickup's dents and scratches were Purple Heart tattoos worn with honor. Only 340 of the pickup's 940 manufactured horses' hooves were making it to the pavement. The wind noise whistling through the pickup's cracked seals was drowned out by the cranked volume of Roky Erickson's "Two Headed Dog."

> Two headed dog, two
> headed dog,
>   I've been working in
> the Kremlin
>   With a two headed
> dog.

Then the back tire of the pickup clipped the turtle shell and sent the creature skyward. Aesthetically speaking the spinning shell and the flight's arc was something to behold. Cinematic is the word which comes to mind. The spin and the arc were worthy of being projected on the screen of Newport's Roxy Theater. People would pay money for a seat, settle down in that air conditioned comfort, the atmosphere which has not changed since 1951, and marvel at the slow motion, directorial choice. Maybe it's the backward somersault after a body has been shot in *Last Man Standing*. Or maybe it's the tossed bone dissolved into a space satellite in *2001, A Space Odyssey*. The fact is that the soaring of that end-over-end turtle shell was quite a sight.

After reading about the turtle's waterloo in the Dream Fishing the Little Spokane

Library, I left. I walked back through the Dartford Cemetery to my car and went home. I was suddenly tired, but my body wouldn't have any of it. It just wouldn't settle down. It didn't want to be like the people who were laid to rest in the Dartford Cemetery.

So I took my restless self back out the door. I walked and opened the door to my garage where I keep my car. I popped the trunk and knelt down in front of the grill. I counted the insect corpses on the radiator. I numbered the bodies: grasshoppers, flying ants, moths, and three butterflies: two pine elfins and one particularly pretty blue copper. One of the copper's wings waved at me. It was a white flag of a wing.

WHAT THE BIKER CHICK SAID

A biker chick is talking to one of the bikers
at the Dragoon Creek Campground. Their
encampment is a few miles west of where the
creek joins the Little Spokane.

Dragoon Creek is entering into August,
which is firmly in the middle of what we in
Dream Fishing the Little Spokane call fire
season. The birds, western wood-peewees, red-
winged black birds, and a few quail hidden in
the serviceberry, are keeping up an ebullient
chatter.

The biker chick isn't talking to her
biker, the one she came with, the one the
others don't question, just another one who
happens not to be her biker.

The two stand next to Dragoon Creek. The
little trout stream lies still in the way a
woman's hair lies. Individual strands could
whip about like the mane of a galloping horse.
But on this entering-August afternoon, they
don't. On this summer afternoon, the Horsehead
Nebula has got nothing on the flow of Dragoon
Creek.

The biker chick is getting pretty
animated. Her hands are painting the air.
Right here next to Dragoon Creek, she looks
like a photograph of Frida Kahlo. Look at the
photograph, and the first thing you notice is
that both Frida's hands firmly grasp a cocked
revolver. An ammunition belt is fastened at a
provocative angle across her hips. The sleeves
of her blouse flow on either side. The blouse
is open, vulnerable, her left breast partially

exposed. The revolver isn't pointed at the viewer. Her eyes are.

A red-wing black bird calls from the other side of Dragoon Creek. Soon after the biker chick says, "I know somebody who makes the best Spam fried rice."

Upstream, away from what the biker chick said, Dragoon Creek meanders this way through farms, tranquil, and that way through woods. Eventually you come to the Deer Park Mill Pond. Its concrete dam is a mid-summer's barrier to the stream's headwaters. "Can't get there from here." "What d'ya mean? I can't go no further?" "Nope, just like I said, y'can't get there from here." "Well, fuck that."

Back downstream at the Dragoon Creek Campground, the biker chick has just revealed that she knows someone with culinary skills. Maybe she should put in an application at Deer Park's Asian restaurant. The establishment opened not long ago. Folks laid down bets on whether the new business would make a go of it. Doubters cited the fact that there were no Asian springs to supply a flow of Asian culture. The percent of Asian residents in Deer Park was seventeen hundreds of one percent. An internet search of Asian links to Deer Park yields only the Asian restaurant and a single man who claims to plant gardens inside bottles.

- graduated from Osaka Bonsai-Zen Institute
- worked on micro-gardening for fifteen years
- taught bottle horticulture for ten years
- moved to U.S from Japan one month ago

Maybe the biker chick could begin the interview by offering to make her famous Spam

Fried Rice, the recipe she got from someone
she knows, this someone whose Spam fried rice
is the best. She could say she'd like to begin
on a trial basis, get her feet wet in the
conjoining of cultures here along Dragoon
Creek. In fact, she could write out her recipe
on the back of a Japanese beer mat coaster.

Spam Fried Rice

1 can Spam
1 can peas
1 can sliced carrots
1 egg
2 cups yesterday's rice
handful of wood ear fungus,
    soaked
some soy sauce
some ginger, diced

Cut up Spam and fry in wok.
No need for oil. Spam fat
will do the trick. Put in
some ginger and soy sauce.
Drain and put in the wood
ear fungus, peas, and
carrots. Remove. Fry the
rice. Return the Spam
mixture. Whisk an egg and
drizzle it across the mix.
Eat.

Chances are the biker chick probably, most
assuredly, won't put in an application at Deer
Park's Asian restaurant. Instead, on this
soon-to-be evening in August, her words prompt
memories of Spam Fried Rice gone by. These
memories call her to action. And her actions
result in a fry pan brimming with Spam Fried
Rice.
    As if on cue Saint Francis descends from
heaven on a Horsehead Nebula of a staircase.

Life all about comes to the table. Then, the
meal is served, the dish the biker chick knows
so well, the dish she says is the best.

THE OUT-OF-THE-WAY ALLEY FORGE

Walking down a street in Deer Park one day, I duck down a dark, out-of-the-way alley. I want to escape the oppressive 5:00 o'clock heat. I need to turn down the glare.

What I find is the back of some derelict buildings, the kind which were put up in haste, the kind of flowers which are supposed to attract bees but attract only flies.

I wonder about who it was that put up these buildings. These weren't log cabins. Someone long ago had put in a sawmill and cut the studs and siding. Someone else had melted the sand and formed the glass which later was broken out by some ill-intentioned stone. But whoever put up these buildings wasn't out to impress anybody. They didn't impart too many notions about architectural aesthetics. The back of these buildings, having far outlived their use, sag under neglect and await either a malicious match or inevitable collapse.

I keep on down the alley because these buildings aren't what I'm about. I have no interest in someone else's carcasses.

Ahead of me, under an old mulberry tree heavy with summer berries, I make out what might be an entrance. I say might be because it isn't like one of those lumber company doorways, the ones that come in a cardboard box, that are nailed into place like the head on Frankenstein's chicken experiment. This entrance is an archway constructed of rose vines woven together with carefully chosen deadfall.

Although I have no invitation and because the entrance has no door, I pass through onto a small lawn. I continue over some grass and onto the porch. I like this porch. Somebody has really taken care of it. Not like one of those old derelict buildings. Somebody has arranged two chairs just so. And somebody has hung some pretty curious pieces of ironwork from the structure which supports the overhang.

1: A planter in the shape on an embryo. Paintbrush and shooting star are growing in its soil.

2: A wind chime which operates like a voice box. I listen to the wind play a little song. The night before I had dreamed this song, empyreal, being sung by fish using water passing over their gills.

3: A sculpture. The name plate reads "Testes descending." It must be seen.

4: A cutlery set. The spoons are fish fins. The forks are human hands.

5: Six candle lamps hanging from the mulberry tree. They are in the shape of children's faces. The eyes are wide set, the nose and mouth in between. None has a dimple below the nose.

6: A stirrup. If you put your ear to it, you can hear the future like the young woman coming from beside the building.

This woman wears a paddy cap and is carrying a basket of mountain huckleberries. She asks me if I'd like some berries. "Well, hello, would you like some berries?"

"Why, of course. Those are some fine berries."

"Do you think so? My husband and I were up on Boyer Mountain this morning. Help yourself."

"Don't mind if I do." I choose a single berry. It is sweet, but also with a hint of the earthiness that distinguishes mountain huckleberries from straw or blueberries. Of course, one berry leads to a few more. "I understand you can't plant mountain huckleberry bushes in your garden."

"That's true. Why would you want to?"

She has me there, and I go on to say, "I particularly like your wind chime. I had a dream last night that fish were singing the song it's playing right now."

"Oh, that sounds really nice. I'd never thought of fish singing. If I did, that's exactly what I'd imagine. Why don't you take the chime with you?"

"Could I? How much would I owe you?"

"Oh, you wouldn't owe anything. If you like it, it is yours. Stop by again sometime and bring something you think we should have."

"That sounds okay."

A man then comes from beside the same building. He is carrying a baby, and I figure this is the man she already referred to, her husband, and the man she had picked huckleberries with earlier in the morning. He holds the baby in his right arm and sets a beaver tailed dag knife with his left hand on the porch rail.

"Your wife offered me some of the finest huckleberries I've ever eaten. She also said I could take the wind chime home. I'm going to hang it from the eave over my deck. It will catch the breeze out of the west."

"Sounds alright." He strokes his beard while he sizes me up. He must have been working on that beard for some time because he didn't just give his beard a little tug. Instead his stroke took its good old time, a stroll down a country lane on a late summer evening, the wheat harvest having turned the sky the blood red we here in Dream Fishing the Little Spokane think so interesting, so well worth the wait.

When I turn to go through the entrance, the baby coos. I wonder if this baby will grow up to meet Mister White. Then I think about my next visit when I'll bring a huckleberry pie and a story. This one.

BRAUTIGAN'S CLOSET

Born in Tacoma, WA Richard Brautigan was
raised without. His mother Mary Lou used the
words "dirty," "drunk," and "filthy" a lot.
Richard, Mary Lou, and other family lived on
the edge. Soiled photographs left in the
gutter were distilled and drunk regularly.

Richard didn't talk until he has four or
five. He learned to read by studying the
canned foods primer, chapter 1, "Tomato Soup."
Then Mary Lou pulled his roots from Tacoma's
industrial-accident soil. At nine Mary Lou
moved Richard and sister Barbara to Eugene,
Oregon and decided raising the two was too
much. She boarded her two kids with strangers.

Richard often walked away and went
fishing. Almost as often he took his sister
Barbara with him. No one else cared. He picked
green beans and blackberries to survive. There
was electroshock.

Then there was San Francisco. He hung with
Spicer, McClure, and Duncan. He hung with the
Diggers, walked the streets, and gave away
poems. "Here, please, plant this book: sweet
alyssum royal carpet, Shasta daisy, California
native wildflowers, calendula, carrots,
squash, parsley, and lettuce. Read the poems
and then plant the seeds." He hung with
Joplin, Mad River, and good friend Jimmy
Buffet-pollinating San Francisco like Henri
Rousseau in Paris. Richard was an odd duck
waddling through a conservatory of exotic
plants.

In *Jubilee Hitchhiker*, Richard's
biographer takes the road marked private. He

turns right onto *National Enquirer* Drive. After parking his car, he walks into Richard's old home on Geary Street, a place Richard called The Museum. Prominently displayed are Richard's World War II machine gun and an over-sized papier-mâché bird named Willard. Then the biographer opens Richard's closet. Inside is Richard's bondage paraphernalia. Richard would be embarrassed that we have found his silk ties. Everyone knows that Richard doesn't wear ties. He wears turtlenecks and western shirts. He wears vests and peacoats. Pictures have been taken of Richard sporting a scarf but never a tie.

The embarrassment continues when the biographer interviews a number of Richard's girlfriends. Many confess that Richard insisted that he tie them up before making love. They want us to know that Richard was always gentle. Nothing sadistic ever happened. In fact, the securing of his girlfriends' hands and feet was so loosely effected that his insistence, always sweet, always tender, seemed superfluous. Maybe Richard was afraid he would both offend and frighten away the wind.

I think all these things after having made love. Opposite me, our closet door is open. The clothes hang innocently, disheveled like what remains of my hair. Opposite you, our window is open. A breeze moves up the Little Spokane and enters our bedroom. Our scent mingles with the spring lilac blooms. Our children are grown. One fitfully sleeps below; the other sings and swings his ska-soul at a Spokane nightclub.

I'm the one who brought Richard Brautigan to Dream Fishing the Little Spokane, and for that you say I should be sorry. "For Christ sakes he blew his head off. Why do you collect every edition of every book he ever wrote? I just think it's creepy."

Part of what you say isn't quite right. Although Richard never truly came to the Little Spokane, his watermelon sugar tiger has lived just down from the Little Spokane Fish Hatchery all along. Trout Fishing in America Shorty and Viper Bugloss upwell into the same literary watershed. And I want copies of *Dream Fishing the Little Spokane* and *Trout Fishing in America* to rest peacefully together in the minds of those who cross over the Little Spokane River bridge that says, "I pledge allegiance" and "Now I pronounce you man and wife."

But part of what you say is as right as Richard's "Trout Death by Port Wine." I can't deny that all this isn't just "an outhouse resting upon the imagination." It is reality, this quarter moon of your hip walking away.

WHAT ANAIS NIN SAID

Anais Nin came to the Little Spokane River
after an abortion sometime in early 1930. Had
the pregnancy been the result of a union with
her father, composer Joaquin Nin? Recently he
said to her, "What a tragedy that I find you
and cannot marry you." When she was ten, he
took nude photographs of her.

Was it with her husband, banker Hugh
Guiler? She thought him supportive, he a
sturdy palm with deep roots and she an
epiphytic orchid lying in the crook of his
branch, her diaphanous roots hanging in the
humid air. Harmless, she needed him, a water
lily resting on the blue of Monet.

Or maybe it was with her lover, writer
Henry Miller. She felt her time with him
dizzying, swelling with enthusiasm, symphonic.

"Hey, Anais, look at this painting
somebody put out."

"Can't be worth anything if it's in the
trash. Henry, let's go to the *Les Deux
Magots*. I'm dying for an absinthe!"

"Sure, Anais, but I am in love with this
painting, blind, blind. To be blinded forever!
I am already miserable with regret."

Anais was attracted to the Waikiki Ranch
sitting along the Little Spokane River just
below Dartford and just above Selheim Springs.
She thought the word Waikiki dark, wild,
aligned with the yearning of her soul. The
state of her life, a pregnancy and now an
abortion, made her cry out, "To hell, to hell
with balance! I break glasses; I want to burn,
even if I break myself. I want to live only

113

for ecstasy. I'm neurotic, perverted, destructive, fiery, dangerous—lava, inflammable, unrestrained."

Her passion had propelled her from Paris ten days ago. First in a steamship and then on a train, she now found herself transported in a Packard Phaeton automobile. All about she was stirred by the primeval forest of magnificent and virile ponderosa red pines. She passed under the entrance sign

WAIKIKI

and entered the estate. She felt like a winged creature, and she desperately wanted to use her wings.

Stepping from the car and toward the mansion door, Anais saw a man she disliked. His demeanor was reserved, impotent, insipid, ordinary. She judged him a man whom life makes spent. Anais said under her breath, "I am not like him."

The man, Jay P. Graves, introduced himself and welcomed Anais to Waikiki Ranch. He said he was honored to have as his guest such a distinguished Parisian woman of arts and letters. He explained that his ranch was the most modern, healthful, and sanitary dairy in the American Pacific Northwest. His herd was an ancient breed of cattle from the Bailiwick of Jersey. He was proud that the dairy was regularly checked by the state inspector. He described the ranch's thirty bubbling, sparkling springs. He had built the Spokane & Inland Empire Railroad and the Nine Mile Hydroelectric Dam. He had been a Whitworth College Trustee and a Spokane Country Club founder.

Mr. Graves told Anais that after she became settled, she had free rein to explore the grounds.

Anais' response was a lie. She chose to dissemble that she was demure. She thought saying little would give the impression she was deep. She wanted to envelope Waikiki Ranch in her silence, in her naiveté and innocence, in her femininity.

Anais recorded what came next on a piece of letter paper with her Meteore Art Deco fountain pen. She began keeping a diary as a letter to her father when she was eleven and had continued ever since. Although this page has been lost, the description of her experience shows that Anais had the strength and courage to treat the Little Spokane River as a woman.

> I was born a woman, but when I come to the Little Spokane River, I enter it as a man. I lie in the womb of the Little Spokane and gather strength. I nourish myself from this fusion, and then I rise and go into the world, into my work, into battle, even into art. The memory of my swim in amniotic fluid gives me energy, completion.

> When I lie in the Little Spokane's womb, the river is fulfilled, each act of love a taking of me within her, an act of birth and rebirth, of child rearing and bearing. The climax is the moment I rest inside of her.

When she had finished writing, Anais recalled standing on the bank of the Little Spokane. The river's water was deliciously cold and dripped from her like ambrosia from the delta of Venus.

She asked herself whether or not she had ever experienced happiness. Imagining herself

the passionate, quivering belted kingfisher
sitting on a cottonwood snag overhead, she
replied, "Hardly any."

THE DAY WALT WHITMAN
CAME TO INCHITENSEE

Walt Whitman came to Inchitensee one August evening in 1859. He was pretty down on America. He had just been fired from his newspaper job working as an editor for *The Brooklyn Daily Times*. He liked rolling up his sleeves. He liked editing copy and setting type. Now he couldn't visit his editor's desk inside Brooklyn's 12-14 South Seventh Street.

His good friend Ada Clare was his travel companion. Ada had met Walt at Pfaff's Restaurant and Beer Garden on Manhattan's 647 Broadway. They often ordered potato pancakes with sweetbreads and beer. They talked about the need for a Brooklyn Waterworks. They talked in support of the free soil movement. And they railed against mudsillers.

Walt and Ada thought mudsillers were the worst. Just a year before South Carolina Senator James Henry Hammond gave a speech before Congress.

> In all social systems there must be a class to do the menial duties, to perform the drudgery of life. That is, a class requiring but a low order of intellect and but little skill. Its requisites are vigor, docility, fidelity. Such a class you must have, or you would not have that other class which leads progress, civilization, and refinement. It

> constitutes the very mud-sill of
> society and of political
> government; and you might as well
> attempt to build a house in the
> air, as to build either the one or
> the other, except on this mud-
> sill.

Hammond went on to quote Cicero, "*lex naturae est*," in support of slavery. Hammond also quoted God, "the poor ye always have with you." Walt and Ada were having a lot of trouble with Cicero and God getting all mixed up in this. The mudsillers really were blowing out the candle of Walt and Ada's naturally cheery dispositions.

Walt and Ada were travelling to Spokane Country on a three-board freight wagon. Ada sat between Walt and the wagon driver on an elevated bench. As they rattled along an age-old trail, Ada held her newborn son Aubrey. Aubrey was a Parisian-American love child. He grew in the swirl of his mother's wit and cigarette smoke and was dubbed "the infant Prince of Bohemia." He was the pig iron in Ada's Bessemer furnace. The winds of suffrage, unbridled passion, and free soil blew through him. Just like that Aubrey became part and parcel of America's intercontinental rails, bridge beams across the Mississippi, and skyscraper girders.

"This here's y'r stop. Got this load t'deliver t'Harney's Depot up North. Pick y'up on the way back. I'm gettin' a load o'farina at Fort Colvile," the wagon driver said. They had come to a stop at the edge of the Spokane River.

Walt swung himself from the wagon's elevated bench. He used the top board as a pivot and made a quarter turn in the air. He landed firmly on both feet, elegant like a

four pound blacksmith's hammer, punching up a
puff of trail dust.

If this was the end of the road, then Walt
embraced his duty to care for mother and son.
He reached for Aubrey, and Ada handed the
infant down. Aubrey was swaddled like Jesus
tucked in a fortune cookie. The message read,
"You are a law unto yourself."

Walt then extended up his free hand, and
Ada took it in mock gentility. Her dismount
had a ballerina's flair. The way she
maneuvered her skirts reminded Walt of Fanny
Elssler. He had seen Fanny dance the Spanish
inspired *Le Diable Boiteux*. He had lingered
over the many published engravings she had
inspired.

On the other side of the river sat a
number of tule mat tepees. A single line of
camp fire smoke rose and then feathered out to
the east. A number of dogs came to the
riverbank on a dead run. Their barks were a
mixture of alarm and greeting. A few women
with their children came from behind the
teepees to investigate the commotion. Two
young men positioned themselves between the
dogs and the women with their children.

An older man nimbly hopped from the bank
and splashed his way across the Spokane River.
His squat legs worked powerfully against the
current. He was clearly familiar with this
crossing. He cut this way, confident, then
that way to take advantage of gravel bars and
larger rocks. When he emerged, he shook off
water in the way river otters do, not the way
dogs do in a full-bodied violent shiver, but
instead in a short burst from only his
shoulders.

And then there was a silence along the
Spokane. Unlike in New York, no one took a
daguerreotype of the empty space between the
two men. No one recorded Birth and Death
locked in a wrestling match. Birth had the

119

upper hand with Death firmly in a turtle. Then came Death's moment, the classic switch-reswitch-step over, and Death had Birth just where Death wanted Birth, right where Death had planned all along. Inexperience never reads a poker face. Overconfidence always shows its hand too soon.

Because he was always, temporarily, the optimist, Walt extended his hand. He didn't step, that move might have been interpreted as aggressive. That step might have gotten Ada, Aubrey, and the wagon driver in trouble, the same driver who, just as Walt extended his hand, clucked and snapped the reins, the same driver who was turning his team about, the same driver who was getting back on his way to Harney's Depot.

"Walt Whitman. I've come a long way, all the way from New York. Do you know New York?"

The older man stood silently, and in that continuing silence, Walt remembered hating the word Indian. He remembered boisterously arguing for the word aborigine. He wrote in one of his notebooks against words being "misapplied & wrench'd from their meanings." He liked the word ab*origine* because it was a leaf on the word *original*'s family tree. He wrote in one of his notebooks about plans to write "a poem of the aborigines" with "every principal trait, and name."

Then again because he was always, temporarily, the optimist, Walt took a further risk. This time he did stride, tentatively so, testing the space in between, feeling out the older man's body language, waiting for an involuntary twitch, a harbinger of disaster.

As the fifteen or so feet closed, the older man found that Walt was a half foot taller. He noted that Walt's full beard was graying. A broad-brimmed, wool felt hat sat firmly on Walt's head, cocked just to the right side.

120

"I am Garry. Why have you come? I see you have brought your wife and baby."

"Oh, yes, she's not my wife. The baby's hers but not mine. We have come to see this free, fresh, and savage land."

Garry did not respond.

"And you are *Chief* Garry? I've heard that wherever you go people want you to like them, touch them, speak to them, and stay with them."

Again Garry did not respond.

"We were hoping that you might let us stay with you and your people for awhile. The wagon should return in a few days' time."

This time Garry spoke, but only while keeping his eye on Walt and at the same time watching in the periphery mother and child pick snowberries from a nearby bush. "I'm of two hearts about this. My bad heart is a little larger than the good. Now I am thinking if you are a Frenchman and have our land written down on a paper, you should go away."

"Oh, no, we aren't interested in agreements on paper. We don't want to be held together by lawyers. I believe that much unseen is here. I believe you have many profound lessons to teach."

Again Garry spoke, but only after noting Walt's linen shirt and only after hearing a squirrel scold Ada and the infant for coming too close. "My good heart is smaller than the bad. Soldiers have killed some of our young men and burned last year's grain. The old ways have kept us, the chinook and the camas."

"But we've come to these paths untrodden only to collect, dispense, and sing. We want to traverse the garden, the world."

Garry thought Walt a strange man. He thought all white men strange. They could be lone starving coyotes. These were dangerous because there was no telling what desperation might bring. They could instead be yearling

wolves in a new territory. These were also
dangerous but for a different reason. What
they said and did was too often thoughtless
and rash.

Garry concluded that Walt was neither of
these. Maybe Walt was like the white man David
Douglas who visited Garry while Garry was at
the Red River School, a strange place his
father had sent him. Douglas told Garry that
he had visited one of Garry's fishing
encampments, the one between the big river and
another smaller river. After Garry returned
from the Red River School, people remembered
that Douglas listened more than he talked.
They said that Douglas walked out with women
and children to dig up roots. Douglas wrote
down the way women made moss bread. Douglas
also left behind a son, David Finlay, Josette
Finlay's son, Jaco Finlay's grandson, the Jaco
Finlay who built Spokane House, the Hudson Bay
Company outpost, its log buildings now
decaying not far from where they stood. Garry
heard David Finlay had been killed some ten
years before by Blackfeet in Flathead country.
Garry remembered talking with David. He and
David Finlay liked to talk together, back and
forth in Salish and then in English, so that
it became their own game.

Be that as it may, Garry knew it was never
to his advantage to treat a white man poorly.
He responded to Walt this time more quietly,
drawing Walt a little closer, not only
creating a sense of intimacy but also allowing
the sound of the flowing river to swallow his
words before they reached the far shore.
"These troubles are on my mind all the time,
and I will not hide them. You have a strange
way of speaking. If you talk to me to make
peace, I will do the same to you. Walt and his
friend and her baby may follow me across the
river. You may stay until the wagon returns.

We will eat, and we will talk. We will decide what comes next."

The time for words done, Garry motioned for Walt and Ada to follow. Walt took Aubrey. His strength and height was a bet against the infant being swept downstream. Ada took charge of her skirts. If they filled with water, her adagio would be no counter to the added ballast.

Garry waded slowly in. It wasn't clear how his guests might fare. As it turned out, Garry was right to take it easy. Walt and Ada found entering the Spokane River to be quite a shock. Even in September, the cold took their breath away.

All went well until they came close to Garry's encampment. Here Ada lost her footing. So much conspired against her: the algae-covered rocks, the river's current, and her water-soaked skirts. Her feet went first. Her head and outstretched arms then followed. When her head bobbed to the surface, she was able to spot and then grab a tree branch attached to a submerged tree.

Garry wasn't surprised that Ada was being baptized in the river. He remembered his own baptism at fourteen under strange hands and words. Only the water had been familiar. Today, Garry dove after Ada, put two hands about her waist, and stood. He lifted her toward the bank and set her against the wall of soil and roots. She took no time gathering her wits and scrambling up to safety.

Garry didn't follow Ada. Instead he fell back from the bank and out into the current. The river was deep enough that he could bob if he didn't straighten his legs. He was in his element, the river of his childhood and his manhood.

All the while, Walt cradled Aubrey in one arm and watched the interaction between Ada and Garry. Walt hated to admit it, together the two brought *The Song of Hiawatha* to mind. He didn't care for the fact that he liked Ada playing the part of Minnehaha. He knew that Ada would laugh that hearty laugh of hers if he told her of the dramatic connection. He recalled that *The Song of Hiawatha* and his own *Leaves of Grass* had been published in the same year. Walt's own mother said she had trouble reading both, that they were pretty much the same muddle, but since people considered Longfellow's book to be a poem, she supposed that her son's book must be one, too.

Soon enough Garry showed a toothy smile, emerged from the river, and joined Walt, Ada, and Aubrey. The dogs converged and made a ring, their ears back yet their tails wagging. As they read Garry's body language, their ears came forward and their barks turned to yips. The timid ones gathered behind Garry for protection. The bold sniffed at the strangers' ankles. The youngest lost interest and jumped at one another, one ball of three dogs rolling off into a stand of currants.

Garry motioned for Walt and Ada, Aubrey now returned to his mother, to enter his encampment. As the newcomers walked, Garry, in control, followed. The younger men parted, creating both a safe passageway and a defense. The children, like the dogs, darted in and out in accordance with their individual natures. The women stood in clumps like bunch grass. The bunches murmured among themselves. They needed to determine how to care for these strangers. They wanted to know why Garry helped these strangers cross the river.

Garry led Walt and Ada to a downed log where Walt and Ada sat. Garry did not sit on the log, instead resting on his haunches. The men then stood together like clumps of bunch grass and also murmured among themselves. They needed to determine whether or not they should support Garry's plans for these strangers.

Each had his own theory as to why Garry helped these strangers cross the river.

From this point forward those in Garry's encampment at the confluence of the Spokane and Little Spokane Rivers, the area where generations of Garry's people fished for salmon and trout, the site from where George Simpson removed the Hudson Bay trading post, the location from where Garry, age fourteen, directed by his father, had left for the Red River School over a thousand miles away, and the home where so many of Garry's ancestors were buried, began to return to their daily tasks.

To pass the time Walt sat quietly, listening and cataloguing his observations:

> I am part and parcel of all I
> see—a glorious chaos—the dogs, the
> children, never underfoot—the
> young watching, doing with the
> old—a constant chatter and
> cacophony—a vitality—a Brooklyn of
> aborigines
>
> The gun cleaning—the octagonal
> 30 inch blue barrel, "London,
> 1847" stamped on top near the
> breach—the lock plate, the sitting
> fox in a circle stamped below the
> pan—the cock with its cock screw,
> the flint with its upper jaw and
> flint screw—the frizzen—the
> battery spring—the pan—the
> oversize trigger guard—the
> trigger—the gun stock split with
> rawhide repair, the serpent side
> plate
>
> The men—who go north with
> fishing spears and baskets—who,
> bulged at the brows, are broad-
> breasted and strong-shouldered—who
> return with brimming baskets—with

twenty and thirty pound fish—with
fifty pound fish
     The fishing spear—the point of
sharpened deer horn, the wooden
frame with black, pine-pitch
coating—the hemp line, two foot
and stoutly braided—the eight foot
shaft, mountain ash straightened
with sandstone
     The women—who clean and cut
the fish—who, well-muscled, are
beautiful and vigorous—who put
the fish planks on drying racks—
who make a hearty dinner with
fire-heat rocks—with water-filled
baskets—with loose fish pieces
     The tule mats—tule-drying—
tule-cutting to length, the blade
a sharpened brass gun butt plate—
tule-soaking—tule-plaiting, the
weft crossing over and under the
warp—the tule-rolling—the tule-
unfurling across the lodge pole
frame

Like Walt Garry did not engage in any of
the activity. He remained on his haunches. He
wondered if Walt was a salamander. The little
amphibian had taken up residence in a rotten
log, and the wood had just been thrown on a
fire. Clearly the time had come to break
cover. "Walt, you are a man who likes to
think. You are a man who thinks before he
does. I have no objection to that. I want to
show you a place tomorrow which you can think
about. If you like our tule weaving, you will
find this place interesting."
     A woman then approached Walt and Ada. She
was carrying a basket. She presented the
basket to Walt and Ada. Peering over the rim,
Walt and Ada saw a loaf of roughly sliced
bread.

"This is my daughter, Nellie," Garry said. "The bread was made from our wheat. The Indians planted and harvested the wheat and ground and baked the bread. You whites think we Indians are dull headed, but if I have the business to do, I can fix it. Because I think your hearts have peace, I give you our bread."

Initially Walt was speechless. The humble loaf—the rude willow basket rimmed with serviceberry—the heart-felt gesture—all drilled a deep well. He dropped a bucket past his observations, past his memoires, past his reflections. Finally he hit the aquifer from where he hoisted poetry, "Ada and I thank you for the hospitality. The resurrection of the wheat appears when I recline on the grass. Every spear of grass rises out of what was once a catching disease. The earth renews with such unwitting looks, its prodigal, annual, sumptuous crops."

Evening moved to nightfall and soon enough the sun rose. The dogs and small children were first to be up and about. Aubrey called to Ada, and she responded by offering her breast. Garry, other adults, and Walt were next to wake and stretch, the sun rising in the East like European settlers. Today the sun would move across the landscape, touching everything.

Garry brought Walt and Ada a piece of dried salmon and a large cake. Walt and Ada found the salmon to be strong stuff for breakfast. Garry called the cake "cowish." The cake reminded Walt and Ada of the biscuits they had eaten during their journey, but this biscuit clearly was made from foreign flour. The biscuit tasted unfamiliar, an albino horse in the herd.

"Walt, it is time to go to that place I want to show you. When you see it, you will have much to think about."

127

Ada nodded to Walt. She was fine being without him at the fishing encampment. Walt admired Ada for her independence. She was restless and wary with the customary, but assertive and composed with the strange. Garry gave no thought to leaving Ada and Aubrey with the other women and children.

The path led toward the rising sun and away from the Spokane River. Soon enough Garry and Walt waded through knee-deep shallows on the Little Spokane River and followed the north shore. Like most river trails, the terrain was varied. The men pushed their way through thickets of snowberry and willow overtopped by cottonwood. Mosquitoes descended upon them because the fall frost was still a week or two away. At times the trail ascended from the bottomland onto a drier bench of bunch grass and currants overtopped with ponderosa pine. Walt noticed scat left behind—a hair and bone cigar-roll—glistening olives—a watery crowberry and fish pile.

The men spoke very little. Walt took this to mean that the time for talk was at destination's end. The sun climbed and the shadows shortened. Again they crossed a shallows on the Little Spokane prompting Garry to say, "We are close now. The place I want to show you is called Inchitensee."

The men then turned onto a less travelled trail. Again they climbed above the bottom land. They followed a narrow rush of water coming down the hillside. When their climb reached another bench, Walt looked upon a ruin. This was not the Euphrates or Ninevah of the sagas he had written about. The freshly hewn pine had not yet weathered to a time-honored gray. Not long ago someone had industriously built only to have their construction torn apart.

Garry cupped his hands in the rushing water, pulled a portion of the stilled stream

128

to his mouth, and drank. Walt followed Garry's lead. Both men drank deeply, drawing in Inchitensee, refreshing, this blood poured out for them.

Garry led Walt to a place where the rock tripe and rock-shield lichens had been worn away. Both sat and rested, the sun at its zenith. Garry reached into a buckskin bag he was carrying. He brought forth bread leftover from last evening's meal and broke a piece for Walt.

"This," and Garry pointed to the disconnected wood scattered in this place and over there, "commenced when an American named Yantis came here. We call him the American Judge.

"Yantis is a hard man. When he came, he talked to me. We had an understanding to make a mill. He saw that we had farms and grew grain. If we had a mill, we would grind our grain into flour and make bread.

"Then so much happened. The Americans and Yakima were fighting, and I think they were both equally guilty. Some white people were taking too much. Both Americans and Indians spilled blood. I heard Yantis was captain of the Invincibles. He did not talk friendly and shake hands; he wanted to kill Indians for our land.

"Then Americans and Indians were fighting some more. The Americans have drawn a line with Whites and Indians on his side. But Americans and English claim land on both sides and then make a useless war with the Indians.

"When the fighting was done, Yantis came to me again. He said that you Indians are planting your fields. Again he told me about making a mill.

"Because I would be very glad no enmity should be left, I was very pleased. I fix it so that the Indians build a millrace and waterwheel and a millhouse here at

Inchitensee. Yantis brought the grinding stones and machine. The bread that you are eating was made from this mill.

"Now it has gone bad. Yantis told me that Indians do not understand his laws. Because he had brought the stones and machine, our land would be written down on his paper. I thought this business was not a square deal.

"I told the people hereabouts, and they got mad because they did not want to give Inchitensee. When they took the mill apart, Yantis took the stones and machine to the Colvile valley. I am not very sorry for it. Poor Indians again will take their grain three day's journey to the mill at Fort Colvile."

Walt sensed that Garry's story was at an end. The silence opened a space for images and words to rush in. He remembered sitting in Pfaff's and talking with Ada and their friends. There they had discussed the way the American Army had recently destroyed the Seminoles' food supply as a way to force them off their lands.

These thoughts led Walt to remember the time he spent with prisoners in New York's Tombs. Built on the inadequately drained Collect Pond, the resulting swamp and surrounding slum set the tone for his visits. He recalled one time writing the words "damned shame" about the experience, and then he recalled writing many more.

> I become any presence or truth
> of humanity here,
>   See myself in prison shaped
> like another man,
>   And feel the dull
> unintermitted pain.
>
>   For me the keepers of convicts
> shoulder their carbines and keep
> watch,

        It is I let out in the morning
    and barred at night.

        Not a mutineer walks hand-
    cuffed to the jail, but I am hand-
    cuffed to him and walk by his
    side,
        I am less the jolly one there,
    and more the silent one, with
    sweat on my twitching lips.

    The day Walt Whitman came to Inchitensee
Garry and Walt gazed from this ruined place
across the Little Spokane to the bare cliff
face of Rattlesnake Hill. Just one year
before, Garry's people had been crushed. The
American Army slaughtered almost seven hundred
horses and burned their wheat fields. After
treaties were signed, Qualchan, a Yakima
warrior and six Palouse were tricked into
coming to the Army camp and were summarily
hanged. A few days later Chief Owhi,
Qualchan's father, was shot dead trying to
escape.
    And only two months before, the Battle of
Black Jack, the Battle of Osawatomie, and the
Pattawatomie Massacre had culminated in the
tragic raid on the armory at Harper's Ferry.
Soon enough the booms of siege mortars would
be heard at Fort Johnson and would explode
over Fort Sumter. History marks these booms as
the first sounds of the American Civil War.
    Sitting together in the silence above the
Little Spokane River, Garry and Walt were sure
that they had had been hearing the sounds of
the American Civil War for quite some time.

LITTLE SPOKANE RIVER KOAN #3

History tells us that those living at
Inchitenssee were driven off. The powerful
gave the weak a used horse saddle. The place
was renamed Sellheim Springs.
     Mister White likes to swim right at the
spring's confluence with the Little Spokane.

THE LAST TIME I SAW
VIPER BUGLOSS

The last time I saw Viper Bugloss was on a leaf-fall evening along Deadman Creek. I was out for a drive as I often do when I get restless. I usually bring some minimal fishing gear just in case I come across a hole which has escaped my notice. "Hello, I was wonderin' what you were up to. ... Oh, I see, don't mind if I do."

I was in one of my drive-to-Canada moods. Things at home weren't going the way I liked. My marriage wasn't working well, which is to say, I didn't know how to make the thing work. If my marriage were a garage opener, I pushed the POWER button on the remote. Then I started to back the car out, but something just came to mind, stopped me, and I pushed the POWER button again, only this time the door came down, CRASH, and I found myself sitting there with the garage door firmly resting atop the trunk of my car.

I headed out Mill Road, down the grade into the Little Spokane Valley, very peaceful and very exciting, and onto Little Spokane Drive. I always try and imagine away the golf course and houses. Once upon a time the surface of glacial Lake Columbia would have been above me, cold, and once upon another time the great Missoula Floods would have ripped through taking life and limb. At least once lake and flood combined, which must have been quite a sight and sound. "Hey, Honey, I think that tornado and train are both headed

133

straight for us. Fasten your safety belt. Next stop the Walla Walla or Willamette Valleys or, maybe, on across the Columbia Bar and out to sea."

Soon enough I crossed over the Little Spokane River and turned onto Shady Slope Road. I've always liked the name. The word shady gives me peace of mind, which, as I said, I was having trouble finding. I also think the word shady tastes of bittersweet chocolate, dark, a good graveside cry, a remembrance of that time we sat together atop Spring Heel Falls, the time you said those words, that thing you couldn't take back. I didn't drive long on Shady Slope, maybe a mile, maybe less. I crossed a bridge over Little Deep Creek, a trout stream for another day, and kept on going until I came to a second bridge.

Here I stopped my car. I opened the door like I was opening a can of sardines. I just pulled the handle and peeled back the door. I flopped out from my seat, although I wasn't oily at all, and walked a few feet onto the bridge which crosses this little section of Deadman Creek that I like so much.

Unlike many of the runs around here, Deadman isn't a particularly lively stream. Most of it isn't spring-fed. Most of its length is fed by rain runoff and snow melt. Down here where Deadman meets the Little Spokane, a few upwells draw nice rainbows and cutthroats in the late summer through fall.

I stopped on the bridge edge and started looking about for signs of trout. A subtle rise for a midge or late caddis would suit me just fine.

Then this disheveled figure appeared from the shadows, pushing his way through the hawthorn and snowberry thickets which do so well along this bottomland.

Soon enough we stood, I on my bridge, and he in his thicket, quietly like one of Munch's self-portraits meeting his painting called "Despair." I looked for trout. He looked for whatever it was he was looking for.

I reached down and picked up some loose granite and tossed it upstream at the foot of some pocket water.

"Don' got a smoke do ya?"

"Nah, sorry, don't smoke."

"Sheee-it. Don' say?"

"No, sorry, like I said, don't smoke."

I figured this must be THE Viper Bugloss I had heard so much about. Of course, I had no way of being sure. If you ask me, I'm not sure how knowing that you are talking to a legend really improves the situation.

Does it help to say, "So, I was wondering, are you THE Jack the Ripper? I was just curious, seeing that you snuck up on me. And then there is that big, ugly butcher knife in your hand." "Why yes, so nice of you to ask." "Think nothing of it."

We stood around some more. I can't say we were enjoying each other's company, but it wasn't unpleasant either. We were just two guys out who really didn't know how to get back to from where we came. Sure, we knew the game trail we had come in on, but the whole idea of back tracking to a place we had not long ago left just didn't appeal to us. We didn't come all this way just to cry over the milk we'd left out to spoil.

"Huh, don' got a smoke, y'say?"

"No, sometimes I wish I would have picked up the habit. I imagine it comes in handy sometimes, like after you're all done from making love. You feel like you ought to say something. I mean, some really significant feelings have just happened, but nothing really comes to mind. It would come in handy to have a smoke at a time like that."

"Sure does if y'have a smoke, but I don' got one."

"No, don't suppose you do," and I tossed another piece of granite upstream at the same foot of pocket water. When I looked back, only the thicket of hawthorn and snowberry remained.

Finding myself alone, I thought about what a shame it was that here we both were, Viper Bugloss and I, and I couldn't muster a single noteworthy thing to say. I had no doubt I would have been a disappointment to such luminaries as Attila's older brother, Bleda the Hun, and Joan of Arc's baron friend, Gilles de Rais, a serial killer of children.

I imagined meeting the notorious highwayman Stefano Pelloni. He was known as *Il Passatore* and the son of a 19th Century Italian ferryman. On this particular moment, he was in between raids. He was on his way to assault the Papal stage-coach for the third time.

"Nice night, isn't it?"

"Sure is."

"Ever notice how the stars are really bright when there is a new moon?"

"Not really."

PEAMOUTH

Peamouth was the grandson of a Confederate
deserter from the battle of Chickamauga.
Grandpa was a rifleman in the Army of
Tennessee and was twice ordered on September
18, 1863 to charge Alexander's Bridge by
General St. John Liddell, an officer who was
rumored to be pro-emancipation. The Yankee's
Lightning Brigade held the bridge with newly
issued repeating Spencer rifles. Peamouth's
grandpa, who had been a teenage field hand
before meeting the elephant, watched as his
comrades' souls were combed from their bodies
like so many cotton seeds run through a gin.
Six bullets from a single Yankee rifle buzzed
his ear while he feverishly reloaded. Later in
the dead of night, Peamouth's grandpa was
heard to say, "Sheee-it" before diving below
the surface like a raccoon-spooked bullfrog.

   Peamouth's grandpa came to the surface in
and around Tshimakain Creek and Tum Tum. Here
he worked both the fields and the still. He
had a liaison with a Semtaussee girl. She was
born at the Little Falls village where
inhabitants still lived in earthen dugouts.
The Semtaussee might be thought of as Inland
Northwest Native Amish. They thought the
modern innovation of tule mat construction
undermined their traditional values. They were
not interested in assimilating into the fast-
paced horse and gun culture so many of their
cousins had fallen prey to. They wanted to
keep it pure and simple. They wanted to keep
it real. Nine months later Peamouth's pa was
born.

Unfortunately, times being an avalanche, cataclysmic, a wildfire, neither Peamouth's grandpa nor grandma took much notice, and as a result, Peamouth's pa spent most of his time with the yellow dogs. He drifted his way toward the Little Spokane timber lands, hanging around farms and logging operations to lend a hand and make some money. He didn't go into Spokane and get involved in the pay-to-play schemes of the employment agencies. Instead he squatted next to Eloika Lake and scrounged himself up a shack and a still. "Hey, how d'ya think y'r go'n t'get along?" "Oh, I don' know; think I'll just sit right here." "Ain't that a bit precarious? Don' y'think y'need a plan?" "Oh, I don' know; seem to be alright just now."

Which brings us to the subject of Peamouth. Fact of the matter is Peamouth had no idea who his mother was. He had no recollection of his ma, and his pa never spoke of her. Like his predecessors, Peamouth never went to school. He grew up knowing his pa's shack and the walking distance circle of woods and farms, lakes and streams. He learned how to buck hay and how to buck a log. He learned how to snag and smoke a mess of trout. And most importantly he learned how to tend a still. Yes, yes, he knew where to scavenge overripe apples and untended grain, and he was aware he had inherited the family Midas touch. He was more than able to turn base fruit and seeds into 'shine.

His name? Peamouth grew up understanding that his uncommon pucker was congenital. He was born with a cleft palate. Someone, no one told him whether it was a doctor, a blacksmith, or his wank-humored pa, sewed up his cleft. This left his mouth in a perpetual state of kiss. Peamouth's pa did tell his son that he was named after the chub minnow they caught when fishing deeper holes for trout.

From an early age Peamouth could see the clear resemblance between his and the fish's mouth. Obviously there was no reason to be upset. The fish was a peamouth, and so was he.

Just recently Spokane County put Peamouth's property up for auction. For decades Peamouth's shack was just part of the scenery for anyone fishing Eloika Lake. Then came $100,000 homes, followed by $250,000 homes. Now folks are building $500,000 homes and up. Developers noticed that Peamouth not only never paid his precipitously rising property tax but also never had a deed for his property. Osprey, wobbling above in an updraft, no longer rule Eloika Lake.

One day the summer vacation kids were at the local crossroads convenience store buying a caffeine-laced drink. They learned Peamouth's name. Now they yell, "Peamouth, you suck," from passing cars as he makes his way to this farm or that stream. His shack is pelted by rocks from the road. The plastic on his only window is shredded by .22 rifle bullets from a boat on the lake.

Soon enough the Spokane County Deputy Sheriff will come. The sheriff doesn't know that Peamouth and his kin have never hurt a soul. Peamouth's grandpa deserted the Confederate Army before he committed murder. Peamouth and his kin have never been to jail, on public assistance, or complained.

This explains why the Deputy Sheriff is uncomfortable discharging his duty. He has every legal right to serve his writ, put the eighty-five-year-old Peamouth in handcuffs, and slip him gently in the back of his squad car. He is just doing his job, feeding his family, trying to be an alright guy. All the same he feels dirty, a squawfish, remembers his minister's sermon about Jesus forgiving the Roman solider.

LITTLE SPOKANE RIVER KOAN #4

A child was attracted by all the commotion
down by the Little Spokane River. There were
prayer flags fluttering all about. One had a
service berry, another a morel, the last one a
basalt erratic.

He heard an attendee wailing, others
talking, and a band playing. The Little
Spokane River Band was playing their style of
Native-pop-waltz-blues. A few attendees had
joined hands. They were in the mood for
dancing.

"Why is everyone here?" the child asked no
one in particular.

"Haven't you heard? Mister White passed
away."

"Who was Mister White?" the child
followed up.

"I don't know."

DREAM FISHING

THE LITTLE SPOKANE

QUESTIONS

The Little Spokane Dream Police stopped by this morning. They wondered if this book you are reading, *Dream Fishing the Little Spokane*, had literary ambitions. They thought this mighty uppity, to be a book about a place nobody had ever heard of, with maybe the exception of a few crackpots, and what are crackpots anyway but people who ought to remain nobodies, because they don't contribute anything, at least hardly ever.

The Little Spokane Dream Police went on to tell *Dream Fishing the Little Spokane* that it was required to adhere to all the rules to which all literary works, which is to say most, must adhere. Just for starters this little book needed to obey English critic and novelist I. A. Richard's rule #1: a literary work must have questions at the end. "What the hell, whoever read something in school that didn't have questions at the end?" "Not me." "Sheee-it, I had the best damn English teacher there ever was, and everything she made me read had questions."

In accordance with the Little Spokane Dream Police directive and I. A. Richard's rule #1, here are the *Dream Fishing the Little Spokane* end-of-the-book questions.

PERSONAL RESPONSE

1: Sigmund Freud in the *Interpretation of Dreams* wrote, "The virtuous man contents himself with dreaming that which the wicked man does in actual life." Describe something wicked you have dreamt.

RECALL

2: What did Viper Bugloss give to children when they made a sale, and why?

3: Where did the speaker learn about fishing with a shotgun? What does Mister White think about fishing with a shotgun?

4: What did the speaker take home from the Out-of-the-Way Alley Forge? What did he offer in return?

ANALYZE

5: List three or more examples of figurative language. Why the hell can't this writer just say what he means?

INTERPRET

6: The writer has real people go to places they never went and do things they never did. Choose one of these passages and recount the series of lies.

EVALUATE

7: Do you think it's on purpose that there are no consistent characters and plot? Do you think this writer knows what the hell is going on?

EXTEND

8: This is not the only crazy book ever written. If you've read one, describe another crazy book.

BONUS

8: Donny's mom, Viper Bugloss' trailer, and Carl Jung all have one canned food in common. What is it?

Answer: Pork and Beans

www.ingramcontent.com/pod-product-compliance
Lightning Source LLC
Chambersburg PA
CBHW020619120726
47905CB00003B/856